The Baguette Murders

ALSO BY ANNE PENKETH

THE BRITTANY MURDER MYSTERIES
Book 1: The Brittany Murders
Book 2: Murder At The Château
Book 3: The Baguette Murders

THE NORFOLK MURDER MYSTERIES
Book 1: Murder On The Marsh
Book 2: The Bad Sister
Book 3: Play Dead
Book 4: Murder At The Manor

The
BAGUETTE
Murders

ANNE PENKETH

A Brittany Murder Mystery Book 3

Joffe Books, London
www.joffebooks.com

First published in Great Britain in 2025

© Anne Penketh

This book is a work of fiction. Names, characters, businesses, organisations, places and events are either the product of the author's imagination or are used fictitiously. Any resemblance to actual persons, living or dead, events or locales is entirely coincidental. The spelling used is British English except where fidelity to the author's rendering of accent or dialect supersedes this. The right of Anne Penketh to be identified as author of this work has been asserted in accordance with the Copyright, Designs and Patents Act 1988.

No part of this book may be used or reproduced in any manner for the purpose of training artificial intelligence technologies or systems. In accordance with Article 4(3) of the Digital Single Market Directive 2019/790, Joffe Books expressly reserves this work from the text and data mining exception.

Cover art by Jarmila Takač

ISBN: 978-1-83526-973-2

For Mike
"I know who you were"

CHAPTER 1

Ever since moving to France, Derek had experienced an odd sensation of stress after the summer holidays.

He blamed the French. Everyone he bumped into complained about how much they had to do after the best part of a month off work. They tired him out with their incessant chatter about *la rentrée*. He and his wife Solenn weren't even affected by the beginning of the new school term because they didn't have children. But Solenn, being French, had returned from their holiday with a daunting to-do list when he just wanted to be zen.

Derek knew all about stress from his medical career. It had been easy to slip into the role of fitness instructor after giving up his UK practice to move to Brittany. In fact he had a class in less than an hour, at which he was expecting six or seven people to be flaunting their suntans. He wasn't particularly looking forward to it. Some took no notice of his instructions, obviously in the belief that they knew better. Sometimes he had to grab a leg or an arm to make sure a pose was correct. Others were so physically out of shape that they couldn't even bend over, let alone stand on one leg. And he was irritated by the ones who mocked his English accent behind his back. So before the class arrived for their first of the *rentrée*, he needed to relax.

The architect-designed house on the bank of the river outside Carhaix was silent. Solenn had left for work in town about an hour earlier. Derek had already scanned the local paper over a coffee and muesli, and obediently washed his Breton pottery *bol* and plate in the kitchen sink, leaving them on the draining board. He did his stretching exercises on a yoga mat that he laid outside on the patio in the early morning sunshine. He could hear the trickle of water from below the willows as he did three sets of press-ups. Maintaining muscle tone was important at his time of life. Then he stretched out his long, trim body.

He stepped back inside through the open bi-fold windows and went into the spacious living room. The walls were decorated with paintings of little white houses with blue shutters perched on cliffs, and banks of hydrangeas and hollyhocks flowering in gardens.

Derek flopped into a leather sofa and took out his diary. Apart from his classes, there wasn't much going on. He liked having a full week on a page and had never used the calendar on his phone, like Solenn did. He underlined a future transaction so that he wouldn't forget. Then he wrote the letters VJ in a square as a reminder for the next day.

He stretched out his fingers, cracking the joints, which always annoyed his wife, before moving to the piano, which stood against one wall. He was rather proud of his compositions for the annual Christmas pantomime, which their British friends had abandoned since an unfortunate death in the local community. But he still remembered the opening chords of Mother Goose's song. He sang out loud, in full voice, for his own amusement:

> *"I'm old Mother Goose, and I must leave my hoose*
> *Because I'm so poor that I can't afford juice.*
> *My hair is too short, my legs are too long,*
> *And that's why I'm having to sing you this song.*
> *I've got so fat that I can't feed the cat, so what am I to do?"*

He glanced around the room, almost expecting to acknowledge an appreciative audience. In the absence of applause he took out his selection of piano classics and turned to a Chopin Nocturne. It was his favourite, the "Op 9 No. 1 in B flat minor". But after a three-week break, it proved trickier than he remembered.

As he embarked on the piece, his fingers immediately started to trip over each other, as though they were sticky. Was it possible to have too much holiday? If there was anywhere in the world this could be the case, it had to be France, he thought. And still they complained.

He knew there was another reason he felt out of sorts. He'd had a painful conversation the previous day, which still occupied his thoughts. As a former GP he'd been used to people deferring to him. But here in Brittany the French didn't seem to respect his status, even as a fitness guru. His professional background meant that he tried to avoid conflict, and he didn't like rows. So he hadn't expected the unpleasant, even violent, reaction to what he'd had to say yesterday. He'd felt uncomfortable, and something told him that he hadn't heard the end of it.

His reverie was interrupted by his phone ringing. He got up and found it on the dining room table. It was Pippa from the village bakery, who occasionally dropped in to deliver their daily *tradition* baguette, and sometimes a cake. It wouldn't do her any harm to join his fitness group, he thought.

"Hi Derek, how was the holiday?" she asked. "It's tough being back, isn't it?"

"Are you another one who thinks that?" he grumbled. "It was great. But it was particularly hot in Arcachon this year. Frankly, I'm glad to get back into my routine."

"You should have stayed in Brittany like we did," she replied. "Nice and cool and no traffic jams on the *autoroute*. I'm going to be passing your place in a bit, if you want me to drop off a *tradition* for you?"

"Thanks, very kind of you," he replied. "Could you put an extra couple in for us? I'll put them in the deep freeze. Save us popping round tomorrow."

"Of course," she replied. "Although you do know they won't taste the same if you freeze them, don't you?"

Derek laughed. "We sound like two French people having this conversation about food, don't we?"

He rang off and returned to his Chopin. This time he found the necessary concentration to pair his fingers with his brain. He was no longer afraid of the repeated arpeggiation towards the middle that required the greatest attention.

He adjusted his stool to give his right hand more freedom for the dominant theme. He was oblivious to his surroundings as he stroked the keys softly in the final echo of the initial melody. As he finished the piece, he sat still and upright, raising his hands from the keyboard with a flourish. At the same moment, the immovable object of his skull collided with an unstoppable force. His head crashed onto the piano frame before he had the slightest idea as to what had happened to him.

* * *

Pippa knocked loudly on the front door, holding a breadbasket containing five warm baguettes.

After a few seconds she knocked again. She was surprised that Derek hadn't come to the door straight away, as they'd spoken only a few minutes earlier. She looked at her watch. Maybe he was upstairs, or busy on the phone. Should she leave the baguettes on the doorstep? She had to get back to the bakery before the lunchtime rush, as she'd left her apprentice, Gwen, in charge.

She decided to check the back entrance. She went round the side of the house, surrounded by grass and trees which gave an artful impression of having been carelessly laid by nature.

A yoga mat lay on the terrace. Pippa noticed that the folding doors were open and stepped into the living room.

The first thing she saw was Derek leaning over the piano. Then she noticed the dark blood dripping from his head onto his sheet music and all over the keys.

Her first instinct was to scream. She dropped the breadbasket onto the stone floor and ran to him, wondering what to do. She took out her phone in panic and instinctively rang her friend Jennifer. She would know what to do. But when Jennifer answered the phone, Pippa could hardly get her words out.

"It's Derek," she stammered.

"What about him?" said Jennifer, her voice tinged with concern. "Has something happened?"

"I think he might be dead!"

Pippa explained about the baguette delivery and how they'd spoken less than half an hour ago, her words tripping over each other.

"So he's unconscious?" said Jennifer.

"Yes. Definitely. Should I try to find a pulse? Help me, Jennifer, I don't know what to do!" Pippa's stomach was churning. She stretched out a hand towards Derek's motionless body, then jumped back in fright. It seemed to her that he was still warm.

"Call the emergency services. Dial 15. I'm coming straight over," said Jennifer.

Pippa was shaking all over. Haltingly, she replied to the questions on the other end of the line and was told that paramedics were on their way. She suddenly remembered that the first person she should have informed was Solenn, who answered the phone at the dental surgery in clipped tones until she recognised Pippa.

While she waited for help to arrive, Pippa dared to approach Derek again for a closer look. She wondered whether she should call the gendarmerie. Her instinct told her not to ring Yann. She knew that the fact that she was in a relationship with a gendarme meant that she should avoid that at all costs. The last thing she wanted was to embarrass him professionally, particularly as she was the one who'd found Derek. The medics would ring the police if necessary, she thought.

Then she noticed something odd about Derek. At first glance, he seemed to have dandruff on the shoulders of his dark sweater. But on closer inspection, Pippa realised that the white stuff was in fact . . . breadcrumbs.

CHAPTER 2

The paramedic who examined Derek, still twisted over the piano, turned to Pippa.

"He's gone," he said, with a sorrowful shake of the head. He pulled down his lips in a Gallic expression, which gave her to understand that Derek hadn't stood a chance. He took out his phone and had a rapid-fire exchange with somebody.

"The gendarmes are coming," he said. "The prosecutor will have to decide about an investigation."

That didn't help to assuage Pippa's feelings of guilt. She shifted her feet from one to the other, aware that time was passing and that she had to get back to the bakery. But now the gendarmes were on the way, she'd have to wait.

She heard a car door slam followed by the sound of the front door opening. Solenn, a petite, birdlike figure with a beak for a nose, rushed in. She dropped her designer handbag and gasped when she saw Derek. Pippa had to hold her up to stop her falling over beside the body.

"What happened?" Solenn asked her.

"His skull was fractured," said the paramedic. "I'm so sorry."

"So he was attacked here, in our own home?" Solenn screamed.

The sound of loud knocking on the front door interrupted her, and she went to let in two gendarmes, a man and a woman, in uniform. Pippa was relieved to see that the male officer wasn't her boyfriend.

"My husband has been killed!" Solenn announced to them.

"Madame, we are here to investigate. The coroner will decide whether it is a suspicious death."

"But it's obviously suspicious!" she cried, stabbing a finger in Derek's direction. "Look at the wounds, they're on the back of his head. It's not as if he collapsed from a stroke and hit his forehead on the piano. Is it?"

There was another knock on the door and Pippa went to open it. She was so surprised to see her friend Meredith standing outside that she didn't know whether to let her in. But Meredith pushed past her. Her eyelids drooped, giving the impression that she was exhausted, which she probably was. She walked heavily, like a clipper swaying on the ocean swell, although without the stick that indicated she was suffering from one of her periodic attacks of gout.

"What are you doing here? There's been—" Pippa began.

"I know, dear," said Meredith. Her voice was tremulous, lacking her usual authoritative tone. "The SAMU called me about Derek. In my official capacity as mayor of the *commune*, you understand. Where is he, the poor dear?"

Pippa stepped back and gestured towards the living room. She watched Meredith make her way into the room where their friend was slumped over the piano. Then she went into the kitchen to make a cup of tea for Solenn as the house began to fill up. A man who introduced himself as the coroner examined the body at length before holding consultations on the phone and with Meredith, who was filling out forms, her face drained of all colour. A man in white overalls took photographs. When Pippa emerged from the kitchen, the paramedics had gone. Meredith left after enveloping Solenn in a bear hug and blowing a kiss to Pippa. Then another team arrived and carefully removed the body.

One of the gendarmes, a woman who introduced herself as Maguy Gallou, *maréchal des logis-chef*, approached Pippa, who eyed her warily. She'd never heard of such a fancy title.

"Are you a witness?" the gendarme asked. She noticed the loaves of bread on the floor. "Do you know what these baguettes are doing here?"

A red flush flooded over Pippa. Had the gendarmes also noticed the breadcrumbs on the body?

"I have a bakery in Louennec. I . . . er, I just dropped in to leave some *traditions* for him and Solenn," she stammered, looking to Solenn for help. But Derek's wife was sipping her tea while answering questions from the other officer, who was taking notes.

"When I arrived, I was surprised that he didn't answer the front door. You see, I'd called him to offer to deliver the bread." There would be a record of that call on Derek's phone, she thought. But what would that prove? She began shaking again. *Did they think that she was the murderer?* Maguy Gallou looked up from her notebook.

"Are you alright, Madame? Do you want to sit down?"

"Well, I do have to get back to my bakery," said Pippa. "My apprentice is on her own, and she needs me."

They heard the front door close and Jennifer walked in. Everyone turned round. *Thank goodness*, thought Pippa. She watched her friend walk straight over to Solenn. "I'm so, so sorry," Jennifer said, putting a comforting arm round Solenn's shoulder.

Then she did the same with Pippa, asking her whether she was OK. "You look like you've seen a ghost," she added.

Pippa introduced her to Maguy Gallou. "This is our friend Jennifer. All the English in the village know— I mean, knew, Derek."

"Madame, excuse me, but you were just saying that you were surprised he didn't answer the front door," said the gendarme. "So how did you get in?"

"Through the back." Pippa gestured towards the bi-fold windows. "The doors were open."

"And was Monsieur already dead when you came in?"

Pippa was breathing in short, nervous spurts. *Is this what a heart attack feels like?* she wondered.

"I was so surprised to see him like that, I didn't know whether he was dead or not. I panicked," she said. She felt a drop of sweat slowly slipping down her forehead, but didn't dare brush it away.

Jennifer interrupted. "Pippa rang me. I told her to dial 15."

The gendarme nodded slowly. "I see," she said.

Pippa was reminded of Yann, who rarely expressed an opinion during an investigation, so it was impossible to know what he really thought.

They could hear laughter from the back garden. Three people, holding yoga mats, were standing outside. They stopped laughing as soon as they saw the gendarmes in uniform.

"Oh no!" Solenn exclaimed. "They're here for Derek's exercise class!"

CHAPTER 3

Pippa dreaded returning home that evening.

She presumed that Yann would have heard about *l'Anglais* found dead in his living room, and maybe even the detail that she was the one who'd discovered the body.

Her last customer at the bakery was Madame Briand, an elderly lady who lived behind a white fence on the other side of the street. She was in her eighties — at least — but dressed elegantly and refused help to cross the street when she left the shop. Pippa felt sorry for her as she lived a solitary life, and always lingered while she made up her mind to take her usual demi-baguette.

After wishing Madame Briand a *bonne soirée*, Pippa finished wiping down the counter, turned the *"ouvert"* sign on the bakery door to *"fermé"*, and waited for the metal grille to come down. She still took pride in the lettering on the window which proclaimed her to be *"Artisan Boulanger"*. It had taken blood, sweat and tears to get her diploma, lease the bakery and fund its renovation. But after her mid-life career change she still had no regrets about becoming her own boss, except for having to get up at 4 a.m. every morning.

It took her only a couple of minutes to walk round the corner, past the *mairie*, to the quiet cul de sac where she and Yann were next door neighbours.

She noticed that his Peugeot was in the drive. Steeling herself, she rang his doorbell. He opened the door straight away, standing in the hallway in jeans, a T-shirt and bare feet. His shaven head, smooth as silk, glistened under the hall light.

"I just got home," he said. "Come in."

Pippa hesitated. "Have you heard?"

"You mean about *l'Anglais*? Of course," he said, holding out a hand. She stepped inside and they kissed, twice on each cheek. "It's awful. Solenn must be very distressed."

"Not just that," she said quickly. "I mean about the breadcrumbs."

"Breadcrumbs? What are you talking about?" he said, a crease forming between his dark eyebrows.

He led her into the kitchen and offered her a glass of wine, which she accepted. He took out a bottle of the local Gros Plant and poured them both a generous amount as they pulled up two chairs at the table. Pippa explained what she'd seen on Derek's pullover.

"So you were there?"

"Not when he was killed, no. But I was the one who found the body when I went round to give him some baguettes!" The words streamed out and she began sobbing uncontrollably. Yann got up to comfort her.

"I'm so sorry you had to see your dead friend. That's tough." He wrapped an arm round her.

"But don't you see? The way your colleague questioned me I felt she suspected that I might be the murderer!"

Yann burst out laughing. "You mean you think she thought you killed him with one of your baguettes? Was it a *tradition*?"

"Yes it was, actually. But what difference does it make?"

"My dear Peeper. I was joking. Are you seriously saying that you think you can kill somebody with a loaf of bread? It's ridiculous!"

"Is it?" He would know all about the annals of crime, she thought. She remembered the bloody scene. Could a baguette have been the blunt instrument that had battered Derek to death?

She shivered, and looked up at Yann, who was still smiling.

"And even if you were the murderer, don't you think you would have run away?" he said.

He was right, of course. She'd been the one to contact the emergency services after all. But maybe that's what some murderers did, she thought. *Bluff and double bluff.*

"And now, what about some dinner?" he asked. "I've got a couple of quails which can be ready in minutes."

CHAPTER 4

Jennifer's mud-spattered hatchback was packed with vegetables, fruit, flowers and ten fresh chickens when she set off for the market on the following Saturday.

She loved early September, when nature delivered a seemingly endless stream of ripeness, all at the same time. She'd asked the children to help her harvest, while Rambo the ram watched with disdain from behind the gate that led into the sheep meadow. She glanced down the track which cut through the smallholding where the tomatoes were still in abundance in the plastic-covered greenhouse. Trails of courgettes crawled all over the kitchen garden, and the peach tree was heavy with fruit.

"I'm off!" she shouted to Luke and Mariam before jumping into the car. She was running late, as usual, and blew them a kiss. "Daddy will be here for you any minute. See you tonight."

She shooed away Byron, their ageing golden retriever, lowering the window to ask Luke to get him out of the way. The dog sat on the boy's feet to watch her depart. As she checked the rearview mirror she caught sight of her unkempt hair and resolved to make a hairdresser's appointment. She ignored her grime-stained fingernails on the steering wheel.

The market in Carhaix was busy ahead of the new school year. Jennifer's partner Philippe gave her a wink from behind his cheese van, and tapped his watch, noting her tardy arrival. She gave him a shrug, in the French way, signifying, *what can I do about it?*

She began unpacking her produce, glancing round the market where Pippa, who had the stall next to hers, was handing out fresh loaves to a line of customers. She noticed Pippa's rival baker from a neighbouring village watching sulkily from his corner spot.

Solenn's space, where she sold traditional Breton jewellery depending on the season, was empty. Jennifer felt a pang of sympathy for her friend and wondered how she was coping. Despite the stress of the *rentrée* in two days' time, Jennifer had invited Solenn over for a meal once the school term had begun, in hopes of cheering her up.

As she hauled some chickens onto the stall, she heard someone call out, in English, "Jennifer, my dear," and recognised Meredith approaching, dressed in flowing robes, opaque black tights and open-toed sandals. With her tresses of grey hair she looked the part of an Earth Mother.

"I see you have chickens today. I'll take two please," said Meredith.

"Yes. You've got it right. Once a month," Jennifer replied with a smile. "Eggs?"

"I'll take six, thanks." Meredith got out a twenty euro note and some small change and went on, "This is so sad about Derek, isn't it? I can still see his terrible head injury when I close my eyes. I can hardly believe it! I mean, I can't think of a nicer person."

Jennifer nodded in agreement. "And poor Solenn. It's dreadful for her. Are you still coming round for dinner with her and Pippa next week?"

"Of course. But it's a busy time," said Meredith. "We've got the first council meeting of the *rentrée*, and the dreaded Sylvie Le Goff is supposed to be making an appearance."

"Well, I'm glad that you decided not to stand down as mayor," said Jennifer.

"How could I?" Meredith replied. "I'm pretty fed up with the hostility I'm getting these days, as though I'm to blame for everything that goes wrong in this country. But what with losing my first deputy, and then Sylvie being off for so long after her accident, I have to hold the fort, don't I?"

* * *

A couple of hours later, Jennifer and Pippa were ensconced in the corner of their favourite café beside the market for a quick cup of coffee.

"I've got to get back to the bakery, as Gwen's been on her own this morning," Pippa said apologetically. "Saturdays are a nightmare." She glanced towards the bar where Philippe was standing with a glass of wine chatting to Jean-Luc, the market crêpe-seller. "Shall we ask Philippe to join us?"

Jennifer shook her head. "No, don't worry. He knows you and I want to catch up. I'll see him back at the house. We're harvesting veggies this afternoon. The kids have gone off somewhere with Jonathan."

"Your job is never ending, isn't it?" said Pippa with a smile. She called over the waiter and the two of them ordered small noisette coffees containing a splash of milk.

"How are you feeling?" Jennifer asked. "Have you got over your gruesome discovery?"

"Not really," said Pippa. "When you see something like that you can't unsee it. And I can't get out of my mind that the police might think I killed Derek."

"Why on earth . . . ?"

"Because of the breadcrumbs." Pippa's tone of voice seemed almost apologetic.

"But Pippa, how can somebody be killed with a baguette?"

"I've been thinking about it," she said. "What if it was really stale? Or frozen?"

Jennifer leaned back into the leatherette bench as the waiter put down their coffees with a glass of water for each of them.

"A stale baguette as a murder weapon? Are you kidding me? Pippa, there's no way! Forget about it," said Jennifer.

"But I can't forget about it. I saw the breadcrumbs!"

"Maybe the killer was eating a sandwich . . . For goodness' sake, let the police figure that out. Do you think they can trace the flour or something?" Jennifer asked.

Pippa looked at her in surprise. "I doubt it," she replied. "Tristan and all the bakers round here get our flour from the same supplier."

"You mean Bucky?"

Pippa looked puzzled. "Why do you call him that? His name's Tristan."

"Have you seen the buck teeth? I couldn't take my eyes off them this morning when I saw him," said Jennifer, screwing up her mouth. Pippa burst out laughing.

"Oh, I see what you mean. But he's more cunning than he looks. I came back to the market because I was worried that he'd steal my customers when he opened his stall."

"Yes, but you've cornered the market with your *tropéziennes*, haven't you?" said Jennifer, referring to the festive brioche cream cakes from Pippa's bakery which had made her reputation.

"True enough," said Pippa with a smile. "But we all have to make a living and it's a competitive environment. And what with the cost of living going up all the time, like the flour and electricity . . ." Her voice trailed off.

"Anyway, that's enough gloom and doom. I'd better get going." Pippa picked up her bag and stood up. "Can you pay? I'll see you at your dinner for Solenn."

CHAPTER 5

Byron's bark, or rather the strangled sound that passed for a bark through his ageing vocal chords, alerted Jennifer to her friends' arrival even before she heard the door knocker.

Wiping her hands on her apron, she opened the door to Meredith who was sheltering from a fine drizzle under the wisteria. Just as she let her in, Pippa and Solenn came down the garden path. As usual Jennifer felt like a country bumpkin in trainers and jeans, while Solenn had on a figure-hugging dress and heels. For the French, a public space was a place of seduction, even in bereavement, she thought. If she'd been bereaved, she probably wouldn't even bother with make-up.

"Good to see that you're all so punctual," Jennifer said. She gave Solenn a warm hug and kissed the others on the cheeks before they hung up their jackets in the hall.

"I thought we'd have dinner inside. Just as well, as it so happens," Jennifer added. She led them through to the living/dining room where she'd laid the table. The smoky fumes from roasting lamb wafted in from behind the closed door to the kitchen.

"The children are just finishing their tea. The lamb's for us," she added. Then she said in a loud voice, "Mariam, Luke, come over and say hello to our guests."

They heard the sound of chairs being pushed and the kitchen door opened. Luke came over and shook everyone's hand, while Mariam's willowy figure held back. His pallid complexion was in contrast with that of his elder sister, who nodded perfunctorily at the guests. Then, sensing Jennifer's frown, she said a "*bonsoir*" to the women as she allowed them to kiss her on the cheeks.

"Ca va, la rentrée?" Solenn asked her. Mariam nodded, before turning to go.

"You'll clear the table will you, before you go up to do your homework?" Jennifer called after them. The only reply was the closing of the door.

"Honestly. Teenagers," she said with a grin to the others.

"How old is Mariam now?" Solenn asked.

"She just turned fourteen. Going on forty," said Jennifer.

"What do you mean?" Solenn asked.

"Oh, you know, she thinks she knows better than everyone else. And she can't help lecturing the rest of us about saving the planet . . . but she forgets we're on her side."

Everyone nodded in sympathy. "It's the farmers she should lecture about polluting us with their pesticides, not smallholders like you with your organic veggies," Pippa commented.

"Is she in *troisième* now?" Solenn asked.

Jennifer pulled a face. "Yes, unfortunately. She's got the Brevet exams next summer so she'd better get her head down."

"And Luke?" Solenn asked.

"He's ten now," Jennifer replied. "But much more outgoing and confident than she is. Although Mariam seems to have got over all the teething problems that she had when we arrived. It was such a huge change for her, being a little brown girl and all that."

Jennifer didn't mention the bullying that their adopted daughter had suffered at school in Carhaix after their family arrived from ethnically diverse Hackney.

But she added, "The locals don't like outsiders round here, do they?"

At this, Solenn, the only Breton in the room, affected shock and surprise.

"Mariam is very poised," Pippa interjected. "She's growing up fast."

"And they're both completely bilingual, aren't they?" Solenn remarked.

"Oh yes. That didn't take long at all. Unlike me, of course. Although my French has improved a lot since I've been seeing Philippe."

"Is he here?" Solenn asked. She had got to know Philippe better as he was the only other French person in their little social group.

"Only in spirit," said Jennifer. "He's at his place tonight, as he has to pick up some cheeses for a Thursday market tomorrow, but he's contributed some amazing creamy Gorgonzola to our dinner."

Pippa beamed. Jennifer knew she was rather partial to cheese.

"Now, *mesdames*, the usual?" she went on, gesturing to the women to sit at the table while she went into the kitchen in search of some Gros Plant.

They settled down with their drinks at the table, which had already been laid for dinner. Jennifer reached out to squeeze Solenn's hand, the fingernails blood red with varnish.

"How are you doing?" she asked.

Solenn raised a hand to wipe away a tear that had suddenly clouded her eye, and sighed. "Not great. There's so much to do, just when you hit rock bottom. I've lost all my energy and I'm not sleeping. Although my doctor has given me medication for both."

"You took time off work presumably?" Meredith asked.

Solenn nodded. "Of course, yes. But I'm already back at work after the three days I'm allowed. My boss told me that he couldn't spare me any longer because of *la rentrée*." She sighed again. "It's funny. Maybe it's fate. But when we were on holiday, Derek was talking about giving up his work. He said he wanted to stop the fitness classes."

"Really? Why was that?" said Pippa.

"He said it was taking up too much of his time. And if he did that, I was going to stop work too. Our patients are so demanding, and it's always me who gets all the complaints. Why should it be the dentist's receptionist who gets it in the neck?"

"I'm sure you handle it very well," said Jennifer, getting up to sort things out in the kitchen.

"I suppose you've had to notify Derek's family back home?" said Pippa.

"Yes." Solenn put down her glass and began twisting her hands nervously. "I've only met his children once and I didn't even have the telephone number of his ex-wife. They asked me about the funeral but I'll have to wait until they release his body to the funeral home. We never talked about whether he wanted a cremation or a burial. Or even where he wanted to be buried!"

She shook her head in distress, staring into the middle distance.

Pippa got up to put an arm round her. "Look, we can help out with the English side of things," she said. "If you give me a number I can get in touch with his family there. But as you're his wife, it's your decision about a burial. Unless he left instructions in his will."

Solenn shook her perfectly groomed head again. "He just left a handwritten note in a drawer leaving everything to me. That's it. Oh, and a share to his children as well, but I suppose that's going to be complicated because of them being British and living in England. Everything would be so much simpler if only they were French."

Jennifer pushed open the kitchen door and brought out slices of roast lamb and vegetables on a tray which she deposited on the table.

"Smells delicious," said Pippa.

"Thank you. It's one of ours, of course," said Jennifer. "I can't serve it to the kids because Mariam's vegan and Luke got too attached to the lamb. He doesn't see a piece of meat on the plate, he sees little Percy. And of course Mariam teases him about eating him."

"Percy? Was that the lamb's name?" Pippa asked, rolling her eyes.

"Oh yes. They've all got names. We can never slaughter our white rabbit because she's called Lady Gaga!"

"Oh dear." Meredith pulled a face in sympathy. "At least Mariam's not involved in the animal rights movement. She'd be marching round the place shouting, 'Free Lady Gaga'!"

Everyone looked across at Jennifer with a smile.

"But don't carrots scream when they get pulled out of the ground?" Meredith went on. "I mean, this is life on the farm, isn't it? I don't have much time for this anthropomorphism. A lamb is raised for its meat. It's not a pet. And I'm sure Percy will taste very nice."

"Do help yourself, Meredith," said Jennifer. The older woman took two slices of meat and large portions of green beans and potatoes before looking round for the gravy.

Jennifer got up again. "Sorry, I forgot," she said.

When she returned with a gravy boat, the conversation had moved on. She overheard Meredith mention the name of her daughter, Emma, who had recently split up with Jennifer's estranged husband.

"So . . . er," said Meredith, noticing Jennifer's discomfiture, "that's that, then." And she reached for the gravy without another word.

Pippa put down her knife and fork and looked across the table at Solenn.

"Have you any idea who might have killed Derek?" she asked gently.

Solenn pushed the remains of her meat to the side of her plate as though everything was all too much, and sighed.

"My guess is as good as yours," she said. "I hope the police can find some clues. They took his phone, his laptop and also his Filofax. Surely they can find the killer on there."

She gave a Gallic shrug. "And in three days' time we were going to celebrate his sixtieth birthday," she added.

"The worst thing is that he'd already booked the restaurant. We were going to have lunch at our favourite seafood place!"

* * *

The guests got up to leave after complimenting Jennifer on a *bavaroise* cream dessert of mascarpone, Greek yoghurt and her own frozen strawberry puree that she'd put together with gelatine that afternoon.

"Thank you for inviting me," said Solenn, as she kissed Jennifer. "It cheered me up."

"You're so welcome," Jennifer replied.

Meredith lingered in the hall while putting on her jacket.

"I just wanted to say . . ." she began.

"About Jonathan and Emma? Don't worry," Jennifer said. "I never expected their relationship to last, I suppose, but I'm worried about the effect on our children. Particularly Mariam, of course."

"Yes of course you are, dear." Meredith shook her head in sorrow. "I too was surprised it lasted as long as it did, to tell you the truth."

"Really?"

"I've never approved of Emma's taste in men. Since she and Romy moved here, she's had a number of inappropriate . . . suitors, shall we call it."

"Are you including Jonathan in the list?" said Jennifer, with a bitter laugh.

"He's older. Not *that* old, you understand" — they smiled — "but almost ten years older than Emma, isn't he?"

"Well, he's thirty-eight now, a few months older than me," said Jennifer. "But I could see that she went after him. And he was weak." She hadn't meant to say so much, but it was true.

"I hoped after they moved in together that Emma would make a go of it. For Romy's sake. She needed a father figure in Romy's life and I don't know how she'll manage again on her own."

"That's the thing, isn't it?" said Jennifer. "And Romy's the same age as Luke, isn't she?"

Meredith nodded.

"It's always the children who suffer from the adults' selfishness. But there we are," said Jennifer.

"So what happens now?" Meredith asked. "Are you going to take him back?"

"Ha!" Meredith's question reminded Jennifer of a plea from Jonathan that she'd rejected months earlier when his relationship with Emma had appeared to be on the rocks. "Not likely."

"I just think that we'll have to find a way to navigate our way through this like we've done with everything else since we got here," Jennifer added. "My priority is what's best for Luke and Mariam. But so far, we're still figuring out the childcare arrangements."

CHAPTER 6

Two seats were empty when Meredith greeted the councillors who had gathered round the long oval table in the *mairie* for the *rentrée*.

One was next to hers, where her first deputy, Jean-Michel, had always sat. The second was at the end of the table, reserved for Sylvie, who as the *secrétaire de la mairie* was anything but Meredith's secretary. As a long-standing civil servant in the position, Meredith was aware that not only did Sylvie know where all the bodies in the *commune* were buried, but she was practically unsackable.

Meredith patted the chair next to hers and said to Christine, the second deputy, "Why don't you sit? I'm lonely here." Christine, a retired accountant in charge of finance and social outreach on the council, shuffled into the chair beside her. Under her friendly exterior, Meredith had discovered that Christine was as cold as an undertaker's slab.

Meredith cleared her throat. "I hope you all had a good vacation. As you're aware, Sylvie Le Goff is recovering from breaking both her legs in an unfortunate accident. She has just informed me that after spending six weeks in rehab, she will now be taking her holiday, which she is entitled to do, of course. This means that we'll all have to try to keep up to date with the administrative issues that she dealt with."

She looked round the table for support, but some of the councillors from neighbouring hamlets started muttering.

"Yes, Armel?" said Meredith. She'd never taken to the dairy farmer who was hostile to the new arrivals, particularly the English, apparently because they disturbed his cows when taking the footpaths across his fields. In his eyes, the countryside was a workplace from which leisure activities should be banned.

"*Rien*," he said, his furrowed eyebrows making it clear that he meant the opposite.

"It goes without saying that Sylvie's absence is extremely awkward. She's the institutional memory of the *commune*, and if any of us fall ill or take any holiday in the immediate future, we're going to be . . . stuffed." Muffled laughter ran round the table at her idiomatic French. "This is obviously a major problem for small *communes* like ours," she added.

She went on: "But the first thing that we will have to organise in Sylvie's absence is Jean-Michel's replacement. I've been looking at the rules, which say that we don't have to hold a by-election. However, I've discussed with my remaining two deputies, who could take over his responsibility for agriculture and the environment. Christine, Yannick and I have agreed on the candidacy of Erwan."

Meredith looked across at the councillor in question, a young teacher from the village primary school whom she'd championed to undermine the power of the elders who were so set in their ways. He also happened to be the brother of Pippa's apprentice. Erwan grinned in acknowledgement of the nomination, as all eyes fixed on him.

"Now, we all need to realise that because we will be down one councillor, the whole council will have to shoulder an additional workload."

Again there was a low grumbling from around the table over the potential impact on their comfortable lifestyles.

"Is there anyone else who would like to stand for Jean-Michel's position?" Meredith asked. Following her private conversation earlier with Christine and Yannick, she wasn't expecting any surprises. However, a hand was raised at the far end of the table.

"Yes, Thomas? You wish to stand?"

"I do," came the reply. Everyone's eyes were fixed on the retired postman known for his resistance to change. Meredith noticed Armel, the dairy farmer, winking at a colleague. Erwan cringed noticeably. She wondered whether a clique — possibly led by Sylvie in the wings — had put up Thomas to sow discord.

"Fine," she said. "The full council will hold a secret ballot to decide the outcome."

She made a note before proceeding.

"The only other thing on the agenda is whether we're going to apply for the France in bloom competition for the second time, after last year's debacle."

There was silence around the table. The councillors were still digesting the prospect of a ballot between opposing factions for Jean-Michel's role.

"Very well. I thought as much. In the light of the inexplicable opposition to our project of beautifying our neighbourhood in order to attract more tourists and businesses, I think we'll drop it. Frankly, I think that with both Sylvie missing in action and lacking a first deputy for the moment, we'll have enough on our plate for the time being. Any other matters?"

There were none. Christine's head was buried in a file which she snapped shut. Yannick shook his head. The chairs scraped on the parquet floor as everyone stood up and gathered their papers together. Erwan stayed behind after everyone had filed out.

"I'm so sorry," Meredith said. "I wasn't expecting that."

"It's obviously Christine," he said.

"Really? But she agreed with my proposal to put your name forward."

"She's close to Sylvie," he said. "Didn't you know?"

"Well, yes, but I wouldn't have expected such an open challenge to my authority," said Meredith, frowning.

"It's not that. I'm sure that they must think it's *le copinage*."

"What? Why would there be any cronyism? You're obviously the best candidate!"

"Sylvie knows that you are friends with Peeper, who is my sister's employer. And you hadn't heard about the bad blood between my family and Sylvie's?"

Meredith's heart sank. Sometimes the vendettas in their village did her head in. Some of the village feuds among long-standing residents could last for generations, triggered by apparently frivolous disputes, or more often over money or an inheritance.

"Erwan, don't worry. I'm sure you'll be elected. We need new blood and energy like yours to deal with the farming community. Your father can help you, he's a farmer, isn't he?"

Erwan turned to leave. Meredith gathered her things and followed him out, still wondering how Sylvie could be pulling the strings at the *mairie* despite her absence. As she left the building, she caught sight of Christine walking towards her car, where a small dog was yapping through the half-open back window. Meredith called out to her.

"What was all that about?" she asked. "I wasn't expecting anyone else to stand, were you? You might have warned me."

"I'm sorry, I had no idea. I was as surprised as you," Christine replied, her eyes wide in mock innocence. She was a short woman whose spectacles gave her an air of competence that Meredith had always found reassuring. Until now.

Meredith sighed. "I want people to work together on the council. I hate these petty rivalries. Do you remember my slogan when I was elected? *Ensemble*. Together, Christine. Everyone seems to have forgotten that."

Christine didn't reply and opened her car door, pushing the dog out of the way. As though remembering something, she shut the door again and turned back to face Meredith.

"I was sorry to hear about your friend who died," she said. "I was one of his clients. He really helped me with my bad back."

"Derek? Yes, that was very sad. His wife is in pieces."

"Really?" said Christine. "I thought they had an open marriage."

"Excuse me? I never heard that," said Meredith.

"Well, Solenn is French," Christine said with a mischievous smile. Meredith was so stunned she didn't reply as she mentally reviewed the numerous evenings that she'd spent with the couple in the past. How would they ever have the time, let alone the inclination?

"You've heard about *le 5 à 7*?" Christine added, referring to the two hours of the afternoon which the French reputedly spent with their lovers.

"Oh. Yes," said Meredith, not wanting to seem like a stick in the mud. There was no reason why Brittany would be excluded from such a French thing, she thought.

"I saw in the paper that they don't have any suspects yet. What are they saying among *les Anglais*?" Christine wanted to know.

"I've no idea," Meredith said in a brusque tone. "All I know is that Pippa found him at home when she stopped by with baguettes for him and Solenn."

"Ah, yes. The breadcrumbs," said Christine. She gave Meredith a long stare, which left her wondering what on earth Christine could have meant.

CHAPTER 7

It was the end of the first week of term and Jennifer climbed the stairs to Mariam's bedroom with a sense of unease.

She never knew how her daughter would react to a pep talk. But this year would be critical and she couldn't risk her drifting along in her group of friends who seemed more interested in boys than their academic studies.

She knocked on the door before going in. Mariam was seated at her computer in front of the bedroom window which overlooked the front garden. Greta Thunberg stared down on them balefully from a poster on the wall at the bottom of the bed.

Mariam shut down the page that she had open on her screen.

"How's the *rentrée* going?" Jennifer began, brightly. Mariam clearly hadn't expected the question.

"Why?" she replied.

"Is everything alright at school?"

"Of course. Why wouldn't it be?" Mariam's voice had a slightly defensive tone, but Jennifer took it as an invitation to continue.

"I just want to make sure that we're all on the same page, that's all. Daddy will be here in a few minutes to take you into town, but I wanted to check. It's a big year for you."

Mariam swivelled round to face her and waited.

"I mean, after this year, depending on your exam results, you'll either go to the lycée — which will give you more options — or to a professional school, where you'll end up being an apprentice or something like that." She didn't intend to sound snobbish, and added, "Basically, it's important to have options. You've got French and English but that's not going to be enough for a career."

"But I'm only fourteen!" Mariam protested. "Did you know what you wanted to be when you were my age?"

Of course she didn't. Jennifer had fallen into her profession as a photographer but wasn't going to admit that to Mariam. The thought reminded her that the next day she'd be taking photographs of a new-fangled combine harvester for the local paper. The editor's appetite for pictures of man toys never ceased to amaze her.

"I didn't, actually," she replied. "But you might have a bigger picture to think about. I mean, whether to stay in France or go back to England. You might want to go to university there, and I wouldn't want you to close off that route because of not passing your Brevet."

Mariam sighed loudly. "You mean maths," she said. Mariam was a bright girl but maths had always been her Achilles heel, despite — or possibly because of — Jonathan's expertise in the subject. As a financial adviser he appeared to consider maths like a different language, judging by the way he could understand effortlessly the most complex equation or transaction. But whereas his fluency in maths was unquestionable, it had always struck Jennifer that his fluency in expressing emotions was a major challenge.

"Yes, maths," Jennifer replied. "I'm going to ask Daddy to give you some extra help on the syllabus."

Mariam sighed again, and clinked one foot against a chair leg in annoyance. "I don't need *his* help."

"Well, I'm sorry, but I think you do. I know you'll sail through the other subjects, like the climate-related stuff on the curriculum, but this is important, Mariam."

Mariam turned back to her computer and said over her shoulder, "I don't even know where he's living now."

Jennifer approached her and tried to give her a hug, but Mariam twisted away.

"He just needs some time to sort himself out. You'll be the first to know when he's found a flat in Carhaix. It'll be big enough for you and Luke to stay over. Not like the other place with Emma."

Jennifer never liked mentioning the name of her love rival, but there it was. On the occasional times when she'd caught a glimpse of the glamorous younger woman at the market, they'd both studiously avoided the other's gaze. She tried a different tack with Mariam.

"But come to think about it, what do you see yourself doing?" she inquired.

"I want to be an artist," Mariam said.

Jennifer was so surprised that she sat down on the bed. So far as she knew, Mariam was only doing art at school once a week.

"You mean like drawing? Painting?"

Mariam looked at her with disdain. "Yes. It's called art."

"I see. Do you want to show me anything?"

Mariam shook her head. "Not now. No."

"Have you talked to Pippa about this? She paints, as you know."

"No. Should I?"

The sound of the front door shutting interrupted the conversation and they heard footsteps on the stone floor of the hall.

"Mariam? Jennifer?" It was Jonathan's voice.

"Just coming," said Mariam. Jennifer watched Mariam shut her laptop. Then she stood up and asked the question that Jennifer had always dreaded.

"Can you help me find my real mother?" Without waiting for a reply, Mariam went to the door without another word, leaving Jennifer sitting on the bed with her mouth open.

CHAPTER 8

The English contingent from the village showed up in solidarity a few days later for the funeral of Derek, who'd been a popular member of the community.

As a retired doctor, he'd handed out free health advice to most of those in attendance and was well known in the surrounding villages thanks to his fitness classes.

Pippa and Jennifer made their way together into Louennec church, whose stone bell tower shot towards the heavens. The delicate spires of the village churches were a feature of their part of central Brittany.

Solenn, smart as ever in a black outfit, was seated at a front pew. She seemed to have shrunk in grief, and appeared so frail that she might faint. Jennifer presumed that the two young men beside her were Derek's sons from his previous marriage, and wondered if any of Solenn's own relatives had been invited. She looked over her shoulder to see who else was in attendance. Jonathan was standing at the back. He'd been close to Derek, who'd been his golfing partner, although she recalled that the friendship had allowed him to claim to be on the golf course when in fact he was with his mistress. Jonathan was standing next to people whom she didn't recognise but who might be Derek's fitness clients from Louennec and neighbouring villages. *There could be any number of potential murder suspects in here*, she thought.

The traditional Catholic funeral mass was conducted by an elderly priest who spoke in a rasping whisper, forcing the congregation to lean forward on the hard wooden pews in order to hear. Jennifer wondered what Derek would have thought. She didn't even know whether he went to church. Solenn was first to kneel before the altar to take communion after everyone lined up to sprinkle holy water onto the coffin. But neither Jennifer nor Pippa went to the front. A group of elderly members of the community, who seemed to fulfil the role of professional mourners, were already on their knees under the vaulted wooden ceiling, their hands held out for a wafer.

After the burial in the graveyard behind the church in warm sunshine, the remaining guests walked across to the bar-tabac in the village, where Solenn had reserved the small café section. She was given a warm embrace by Michel and Solange, the café owners.

"Please, everyone," said Michel, gesturing to the tables set with red and white chequered tablecloths and where plates of crisp baguettes with ham and pâté were piled high. "We'll take your drinks orders at the bar."

Pippa and Jennifer went over to Solenn and gave her a hug.

"Are you doing alright?" Pippa asked.

"*Couci-couca* . . . so-so," Solenn replied. "It was only after I booked here that I remembered that Derek used to come here sometimes after his afternoon classes," she said in a low voice.

"And was it him who wanted a religious ceremony?"

"We never discussed it," Solenn replied. "He wasn't supposed to die so soon." Her voice cracked and she took out a hanky to wipe an eye. "But I did know he wanted to be buried. So here we are."

Pippa drifted off to the bar to get drinks as a grey-haired man in his early fifties came over carrying two glasses of white wine. "Here you go," he said to Solenn, offering her one. She leaned close to him to take the glass.

"Jennifer, this is Gabriel. Gabriel, Jennifer." They smiled at each other, and he said, "*Enchanté*".

A French couple were waiting to express their condolences and Jennifer stepped back. The woman looked like a dark-haired version of Solenn, with a slight figure and impeccable taste in clothes. She was accompanied by a barrel-chested man who spoke in a loud voice so that everyone could hear how he and Marie-Jeanne had been "devastated" by Derek's sudden demise. She heard Solenn reply that it was all the more devastating because she hadn't been able to say goodbye to him.

Jennifer went to the bar to join Pippa, who was talking to Meredith while looking in Solenn's direction.

"Who are all these people?" Jennifer asked.

"We were just talking about that," said Pippa. "I hardly recognise any of them. I presume that some of them were Derek's clients."

"Or golf partners," Jennifer remarked.

"Or lovers," said Meredith, who could hardly restrain a smile.

"What do you mean?" Jennifer asked.

"Well, I heard the other day, from an impeccable French source, that he and Solenn had an open marriage."

Jennifer and Pippa's eyes opened wide with surprise, and they turned back to glance at Solenn, who was talking to another French couple. "But they seemed to be so close!" Pippa exclaimed.

"Maybe that's what kept the spice in their relationship," said Jennifer, taking a sip of wine. Her other hand fingered the three-legged triskele pendant made by Solenn that she'd worn for the occasion. "Do you think they were swingers?"

As soon as she spoke, she remembered Jonathan and couldn't help wondering what he might be up to now that he and Emma had split up.

He'd disappeared after the funeral and there was no sign of him in the café.

"Does that sort of thing go on here?" Pippa asked.

Meredith harrumphed. "Well, as the mayor of the *commune*, I can tell you that you'd probably be surprised by the sort of things that go on."

Jennifer and Pippa stared at her, then at each other, before giggling. Meredith moved on to grab some food. They couldn't help looking back at Solenn, who was talking animatedly to Gabriel. Had there been problems in Solenn's marriage, Jennifer wondered. Was she flirting with Gabriel over there?

"Do you know Camus?" Pippa asked Jennifer, interrupting her thoughts.

"Which one is he?"

"I mean the writer, Albert Camus," said Pippa.

"I've heard of him, yes, he wrote *The Outsider*, didn't he? But I can't say I've read it."

"Yes. *L'Étranger*. I studied it at college and it's made me think about Solenn's attitude . . ." said Pippa.

Jennifer looked puzzled. "Has this got something to do with what we just heard about her marriage?"

"Yes it has. In the book, the main character gets sentenced to death for killing an Arab. But the real reason is because he didn't cry at his mother's funeral, and his general behaviour after she dies. I'm just thinking, do you think Solenn is upset enough?"

"What on earth are you talking about? She's the grieving widow, of course she's upset! You're not suggesting . . . ?"

"That she killed him? It's possible that she might be putting on a front, that's all. Did you notice how she seemed to think that it was very inconvenient of Derek to die just before his birthday celebration?"

"Get a grip, Pippa! I mean, how can you think that she's not upset *enough*. Define 'enough'. Different people grieve in different ways, don't they?"

"OK. Sorry. You're right. But somebody killed Derek, and maybe they're here in this room!"

The two women surveyed the mourners again. Some were propped up at the bar, discussing local politics, while others scooped up the remaining food from the tables. Solenn was surrounded by villagers paying their respects.

Pippa nudged Jennifer.

"You see that young woman over there? She's my notary. Let me introduce you. She lives here in the village and she did my commercial lease for me."

They exchanged pleasantries with the woman, who excused herself to get back to the office after a few moments. They watched her move towards the door where she shook hands with another couple before leaving.

"Isn't that Bucky she's talking to?" Pippa asked. "I presume that blonde woman is his wife. I sometimes see her at his market stall."

Jennifer noticed the baker's eyes darting around even as he spoke to the notary. She couldn't help staring at his prominent rabbit teeth. "Has he come to steal some of your customers, do you think?" she asked.

Pippa raised her eyes to heaven. "I wouldn't put it past him. What on earth does she see in him?" she added, scrutinising the smart, slim blonde in her late forties dressed in black standing next to Tristan.

"And what are they doing here anyway? Did he know Derek?" Pippa turned back to Jennifer, making it clear that she didn't want to greet the couple.

"Maybe from the market. I think his wife's name is Madeleine," Jennifer murmured. "Did you talk to Derek's sons?" she added.

"Yes, they're nice. But they told me they had to go because they had a train connection to catch back to England. I suppose they didn't know anyone. Probably not even Solenn. Anyway, I'd better get back to work," said Pippa.

Jennifer watched her go before turning to scan again the people in the small café. Was Derek's murderer among them? she wondered, with another glance at Solenn.

CHAPTER 9

Jennifer heard raised voices at Pippa's stall as she was packing eggs into a carton for a market customer.

It was Bucky, unleashing a foul-mouthed invective at her friend. She couldn't hear every word but she could tell from the way he gestured towards his own stall, almost devoid of bread, that he was blaming her.

Jennifer finished serving the customer, and they both looked in the direction of Pippa, who shouted at the man, "Why would I do a thing like that?"

She heard the baker say "Sabotage!" before stalking off. He stood behind his stall and continued to glare at Pippa, who pretended to ignore him. Jennifer's customer gave her a nervous smile before drifting off on her next errand.

"Everything alright?" Jennifer called over to Pippa in a low voice.

"I'll tell you later," said Pippa, with a grimace.

They met up at the Central Café after the market, Pippa joining Jennifer at their usual table in the back. After ordering coffees from the waiter, they settled back into their leatherette bench.

"What on earth was all that about?" Jennifer asked.

"Can you believe it? He accused me of cutting the electricity into his bakery!"

"But why?"

"Jealousy, of course!" Pippa replied. "He said that I only came back to the market to put him out of business. But he must be completely paranoid to think that."

Jennifer grinned. "But you did say yourself that you came back because he was the competition . . ."

"I know. But can you imagine me sabotaging his bakery! And when would I even have the time! I'm up at crack of dawn myself to put my croissants in the oven." Pippa made a sound like a grunt and drank her espresso in one gulp.

"Damn, I should have put sugar in that," she said, putting down her cup. They both laughed. "Anyway, he says he's going to file an official complaint," Pippa added.

"Well, good for him. If someone had cut a cable it would be sabotage, wouldn't it?"

"Yes, but I don't know what happened," said Pippa. "He just marched over and started swearing at me, saying that his fridges weren't working so he'd lost his first batch of the day. I felt that everyone was looking at me. It was awful."

Jennifer patted Pippa on the hand.

"Why do they hate us, Jennifer?" Pippa said. Her eyes began to cloud with tears.

"I wouldn't go so far," said Jennifer. "Look at all the friends you've made. I suppose there's all that resentment that's built up over the arrival of Brits pushing up house prices, the people who bring over workmen from England, that sort of thing."

Pippa didn't seem convinced.

"And as for you, you're better integrated than most of us," Jennifer went on. "Try not to worry about that bastard . . ." she said before casting around for another topic of conversation.

Pippa nodded but her eyes were vacant. She took out her wallet and put down a five euro note on the table.

"Here. I'll get these," she said, getting up. "I'm cooking dinner for Yann tonight, and Gwen will be waiting for me at the bakery."

CHAPTER 10

Pippa walked back to the house that evening after locking up and lowering the shutters. She'd spent the late afternoon in the back room, laminating croissants and shaping baguettes, which she placed in the proofing chamber so that they'd be ready for the oven the next morning.

But her heart wasn't in it after her encounter with Tristan. Instead of chatting with customers who came to exchange gossip, she didn't hover behind the counter and was glad when it was time to leave.

She was in two minds whether to even mention to Yann what had happened. He'd find out soon enough, she thought, if Tristan did press charges.

She took out the shopping from her bag and laid the contents on the counter. It was hard to resist reaching for a bottle of white wine from the fridge and taking a swig.

I deserve a glass, she thought. *Just one.* She opened a bottle and helped herself to a large glass. She could always use a splash in the seafood pasta she planned to prepare with some plump mussels from the fishmonger in Carhaix. Looking out of the window into the small garden she realised it would be too chilly to eat outside on the patio.

She sighed. She'd also bought some *crevettes grises*, which she knew Yann enjoyed as an apéritif with a glass of wine. She felt squeamish at the thought of eating the heads of the little shrimp like he did, but they were so finicky to peel.

She'd just finished setting the kitchen table when she heard the doorbell. She quickly washed her hands to get rid of the fishy smell, wiping them on her apron before going to answer.

Yann was smiling broadly when he came in.

"Had a good day?" he asked. She knew he'd had the day off, which failed to lift her mood.

"So-so," she said. She cast her eyes down despondently.

He hugged her and she pressed herself into his chest, feeling even more sorry for herself. "You must be missing your friend. I'm sorry you're feeling bad."

"Yes I am. But it's not that," she replied. "I'll tell you later. Did you finish your DIY?"

"Yes. How did you know?"

"Because you're a man," she said, grinning.

They went into the kitchen where Pippa served them both some of the white wine.

"*Alors?*" he asked straight away.

He listened intently, stroking his chin, as Pippa told him of Tristan's accusation that she'd sabotaged his bakery.

"And why does he accuse you? Does he have any proof?" he said as soon as she paused for breath.

"How can he have? I didn't do it!" she insisted. "But he's so paranoid that he thinks I'd do anything to shut down his bakery, apparently."

"And you say he's going to file a complaint?"

"That's what he told me," she said. She got up, glad she'd got that off her chest. She'd prepared the white wine sauce on the hob; all that remained was to boil up the pasta and throw the mussels into the mix.

"OK, we'll wait and see if he does," Yann commented.

When she turned round carrying the piping hot plates to the table, Yann was still seated, staring at his empty glass as though searching for clues.

She refilled his glass and topped up her own. They ate in silence for a moment, until Pippa asked him, "What's happening about Derek's murder? I haven't seen anything about possible suspects in the paper. Have you got any leads?"

"It's difficult," he said, pursing his lips. "Keep this to yourself, Peeper, but forensics haven't come up with anything yet. The doors were open when the killer entered and so they may not have left their fingerprints. And we've not found the murder weapon. So . . ." He shrugged his shoulders and pouted. "I think it will take a while. We are interviewing relevant people of course."

Pippa had a sudden thought.

"What about the breadcrumbs?" she asked. "What if the killer was Tristan?"

"And what would his motive be? Did he even know Derek? My dear Peeper, even if a baguette was the murder weapon — which I doubt — it could have come from any boulangerie in Carhaix or any of the villages round here. Couldn't it?"

She knew he was right. They returned to their meal.

"And anyway, have you ever heard of anyone being murdered by a baguette? Of course not," Yann added.

There's always a first time, Pippa thought, as she scooped up a mussel in cream sauce with a spoon. "I heard that you've got Derek's diary," she said after a pause.

"Did you now?" A mysterious smile played on his lips.

"That must be interesting, surely?"

"Maybe, maybe not," he said. Yann's non-committal answers never failed to irritate her. But he added, "We'll have to see what his phone records say, but the initials VJ were in his Filofax for the day after he died."

"So he had a meeting planned with somebody then?"

"That's what we think, yes," said Yann, stroking his chin. "We clearly need to trace this person."

"Well, if you only have the initials, that's going to be difficult, isn't it?"

He pulled down his lips and said nothing. That seemed to be a Yes. Or a Maybe.

Pippa poured herself another glass of wine absent-mindedly. Then she asked, "Did you know that he and Solenn had an open marriage?"

Yann swallowed hard and put down his fork, which was surrounded by a thicket of spaghetti. He raised his eyebrows, hungry for more information.

"Who told you?" he asked, leaning towards her.

"If I tell you, I'd have to kill you," she laughed. "I don't think it's particularly a secret. People seem to think that it's quite common in France."

He reached out a hand to squeeze hers.

"Thank you," he said. "This could be interesting. But if it's as common as you think, it means we'll have a lot of potential suspects to interview."

CHAPTER 11

That same evening, Jennifer found herself listening for the sound of Jonathan's car while eating supper in the kitchen with Philippe.

"Is everything alright?" he asked her, noticing that she seemed distracted.

"What? Oh yes," she said.

They were packing the dishwasher when she heard the Volvo's doors slam.

"That's them. I just need a word with Jonathan," she said. "I won't be long."

She passed Luke in the hall on his way upstairs.

"Have a nice time with Daddy?" she asked.

"Yes," he said, over his shoulder. Mariam was spending the night with her friend Pervenche, whose mother had promised to bring her back the next morning. Slipping on a jacket, Jennifer went out just in time to catch Jonathan before the car pulled away.

"What's up?" he asked. Jonathan never failed to make an innocent question sound aggressive.

"I just want to tell you about what Mariam said to me the other day. It's happened."

"What's happened? Why are you talking in riddles?" he asked through the car window. "Is this about a boyfriend? I'll kill him."

"No. What are you talking about? Can you get out?"

He opened the door and stood beside her.

"This is serious," said Jennifer. She'd not been able to sleep ever since Mariam had asked about her birth mother from Somalia.

"Mariam wants us to help her find her birth mother," she said. "Did she mention it to you?"

"I can't say she did, no. But there's nothing to find. You know perfectly well that it said on the adoption forms 'mother unknown' and 'father unknown'."

"Yes, but I was thinking maybe it's time that we tell her what we know. About her having been found outside the refugee camp in Kenya."

"Are you seriously thinking that we should tell her she was lying on the side of a road when she was found? That might scar her for life." He grunted something before adding, "I don't see what purpose it would serve to tell her anything more."

"Well I think we should come clean with her about what we know. Even if we spare her that detail. She knows that her mother was a Somali, but that's it. I mean, it would start to fill out a picture for her. I think we owe it to her, it's natural that she's curious about her identity. She's asked, and we owe her an answer."

Jennifer faced Jonathan with her arms folded. She wasn't going to give in on this.

"And another thing. She's got the Brevet exams next summer and she'll need more help with getting through the maths. Can you do that at least?"

She couldn't help the tone of voice and could tell he was irritated at being told what to do. But she went on, "I think we should both sit down with her one evening soon and talk things over. Is that OK?"

"I suppose so," he said, grudgingly. "By the way . . ."

It was Jennifer's turn to frown.

"I'm thinking about going back to London. I've not been able to find anywhere to live in Carhaix yet."

He spoke in such a matter-of-fact way that she exploded. "How could you do that to your family? Abandon your children . . . again?" she said. "Can't you ever think of anyone but yourself? You're a digital nomad, what's your problem in working from home like you have since we moved here?"

Jonathan was no longer looking her in the eye. He replied, sheepishly, "Well I've not got any friends here. I'm not like you."

"But your family is here. That's what I'm saying to you. And your children still need you," Jennifer insisted. She tried changing tack, softening her voice.

"Look. You'll feel better once you find somewhere else to live. Luke and Mariam want you around. Why don't you give it till the end of the school year, so that Mariam can get through the Brevet? I wouldn't like her to end up as a hairdresser."

He wrinkled his nose as he thought.

"Think about it, please," she said. "Let's talk again."

Jonathan got into his car and Jennifer returned to the house, wondering whether he might have an ulterior motive for returning to London. Maybe the idea had come from his mother, she thought. It was odd that she'd fallen for two men who were polar opposites in every way. Where Jonathan was physically tall, lanky and handsome, Philippe was smaller, stouter and balding. Jonathan was arrogant and on a short fuse, while Philippe was laid-back and seemingly untroubled by anything. With him, what you saw was what you got. Was he too placid? Maybe, Jennifer thought, but that had to be an advantage compared to the daily dramas she'd had with Jonathan.

Like most French people Jennifer knew, Philippe — who'd not gone to university — hardly ever spoke about work. He always turned conversations into subjects of enjoyment, such as a memorable meal, or a holiday. Unlike Jonathan, who always managed to slip his Oxford education into a conversation with strangers, Philippe's work didn't define him.

He had already cleaned up the kitchen when she walked in. It was another contrast with Jonathan, who'd had to be asked to do anything, including toiling on the smallholding, which he seemed to think was beneath him.

"I'm going to shut the animals in for the night," she said to Philippe, offering no explanation about her talk with Jonathan, and Philippe didn't ask.

"Do you need any help?" he asked, watching her step into her wellies in the hall.

"No, I'm fine," she said.

She returned to the house a few minutes later to say goodnight to Luke, having shooed the hens into the henhouse. She'd checked that the rabbits were safely locked in their cages and the sheep huddled in their shed for the night.

"Just half an hour more, OK?" she said to Luke, interrupting his video game.

"Luke?" she said, louder, having noticed the unmade bed. "I thought I told you about this. Can't you make an effort?"

He took off his headphones and put on a suitably contrite expression, before turning back to his computer.

She crossed the landing to peek inside Mariam's room, where the door was ajar. The unmade bed stared at her in defiance, like the look on Greta Thunberg's face.

"Shut up," she muttered in the direction of the poster before pulling off the sheets to remake the bed. As she was tucking in the bottom sheet under the mattress, she felt a lump in one corner between the mattress and the bed springs.

Lifting that end of the mattress, she found a wad of papers in a plastic bag and took it out. They'd been torn from a school notebook. On closer examination, Jennifer saw that they were pencil drawings. Flicking through them, she saw women in hijabs copied from photographs, Rambo the ram staring defiantly through the gate railings, and the delicate veins of lime tree leaves in the garden. The drawings were good.

There was a portrait of Byron, his tongue hanging out and his adoring eyes looking straight at the artist. One portrait was a close-up of a girl's face, resembling Mariam's, with a black tear running down her cheek. Another one showed a girl with long dark hair like Mariam's and a speech bubble over the head of a figure of a girl standing beside her. It just said "Mariam musulmane". It was the very same schoolyard abuse that had targeted Mariam a couple of years earlier. Jennifer could tell from the dark slashings and intricate portraits that Mariam had been pouring her heart out onto the pages ever since they'd arrived in France.

So this was how she'd dealt with the bullying, Jennifer thought. She was upset for her daughter all over again, but also admired how she'd channelled her distress. Mariam had shrunk from confiding in either parent at the time, although she had agreed to speak with a school counsellor. Then Jennifer had another thought: what if the bullying had started again, more recently?

Her discovery made her all the more determined to sit down with Jonathan and tell Mariam what they knew about her background. But how could they broach the sensitive issue of the drawings? She glanced towards the door before quickly putting them back into the bag and placing it back under the mattress.

Then she pulled the bedsheet and duvet into place before going downstairs to join Philippe.

CHAPTER 12

Sylvie opened the door and limped, with the support of a walking stick, to the end of the table in the village hall where she pulled up a chair facing Meredith.

Meredith wondered whether her dramatic entrance had been on purpose. It could be no accident that the *secrétaire de la mairie* had been the last to arrive for the council meeting.

She made a point of welcoming Sylvie back to work "after a long absence" and expressed the hope that she was fully recovered.

Sylvie picked up the meeting's agenda ostentatiously and scrutinised it as though it was the first she'd ever seen. Meredith looked daggers across the table at her before embarking on the agenda. Firstly, she had to announce the results of the secret ballot to elect the new first deputy.

The sight of Sylvie, her slim frame diminished but her "resting bitch face" just as contemptuous as ever, had caused Meredith's stomach to tighten into a knot. Her teaching career back in England had never been as stressful as dealing with Sylvie and the French villagers who questioned her every decision.

Meredith explained to everybody that Erwan, the local teacher, had won — although only by one vote. He was clearly uncomfortable with the close result and kept his eyes lowered to his notebook. The council had shown, once again, that they were divided, not only along generational lines but also the "townies" against the farmers. Meredith knew that it wasn't just in their *commune*. In fact, a law now protected farmers against so-called frivolous complaints by newcomers about such things as cocks crowing at inconvenient times, and manure spilled on lanes leading to their newly built homes.

Thomas, the ex-postman defeated in the ballot, glanced across at Sylvie, whose expression was inscrutable. For Meredith, it clinched her suspicion that the two of them had been in cahoots with Christine, who smiled at Erwan over her spectacles as though nothing had happened.

After a short discussion of other matters, Meredith ended the session, glad to have defeated Sylvie's attempt at sabotage. She went over to Sylvie, who was taking her time in getting to her feet.

"Does it feel good to be back?" she asked.

"Of course, Madame *la maire*," said Sylvie. "Now we shall return to doing things properly in this *commune*."

Meredith refused to be put off. She continued: "So you see we've got a new deputy. I expect you to give him your full support."

Sylvie reacted by waving a hand in her face and giving a dismissive "*Pff.*"

"I'm sorry, Sylvie, but could you explain what you mean?" Meredith demanded. She was struggling to control her temper. "What exactly is your problem with Erwan?"

Sylvie narrowed her eyes as though it was none of Meredith's business. Christine, the second deputy, exchanged a meaningful look with Sylvie as she passed them on her way out.

"He's the son of Daniel Le Floch," said Sylvie, pouting. Before she had a chance to continue, Meredith interrupted to say, "The farmer? I know his daughter Gwen, who works across the street in the bakery. I'm very surprised that you have any issues with any member of the Le Floch family. I find them perfectly delightful."

Sylvie wasn't put off her stride. She continued, "I am talking about Erwan, the son. He has a reputation . . . but it's not just him."

Meredith couldn't hold back. "And what exactly do you mean by that?"

Sylvie didn't respond directly, but said, "We know that you're friendly with that family because his daughter works for Peeper. And we also know all about her . . ."

Meredith took a step forward, forcing Sylvie to rear backward. "Please explain yourself," she said, almost spitting the words into her face.

"The whole of Louennec is aware that your friend is a police informer," Sylvie replied. She raised her cane threateningly, adding, "Don't tell me that she doesn't pump her customers for information which she passes on to her gendarme boyfriend!"

And with that, she turned her back on Meredith and stalked out of the hall as fast as her walking stick would carry her.

CHAPTER 13

Jennifer surveyed the meagre contents of the fridge to see what she could find for lunch.

Tramping through farmers' fields and trying to get the right shot of a cow, horse or pig was hungry work. She'd accompanied a reporter from *Le Télégramme*, who was interviewing a young dairy farmer to find out why he'd decided to give up a job in Carhaix for an uncertain future working with his father.

Listening to the farmer while persuading him to pose in the midst of his herd, she now understood why his Breton colleagues were revolting. He'd explained that while they received grants depending on the acreage, his father was now staring poverty in the face because he'd lose all that the moment he retired.

"And that's not all," he went on. "We're at the mercy of the distribution chains and the big supermarkets which force down our prices. They've got us over a barrel!"

As they left the farmyard, she told the reporter she felt sorry for them, but he raised his eyes to heaven. "You think that we French are always complaining, but the farmers are the worst of all," he said. "There's either too much sun, or too much rain, and they always want more money. Let's see how long it takes this guy to go back to his other job. *Pff.*"

Jennifer only had about half an hour before Philippe was due to help her prepare some broilers for market the next day in her specially equipped shed which she called her "lab". By now she had the raising of chicks and monthly slaughter of chickens down to a fine art, and was no longer squeamish about the blood and feathers.

She'd forgotten about the shopping on her way home and managed to find some sliced ham at the back of the fridge to make herself a sandwich. She chewed slowly on the baguette from Pippa's bakery, which was crisp on the outside and moist on the inside. As she took another bite, she reflected on one of the most pressing questions of French life: how to keep a baguette fresh? Some people she knew draped a damp tea towel over the bread. It prevented it from going stale by the next day, but then it needed to be crisped in the oven. Others put the loaf in the freezer, either already sliced — which was preferable, although there was a risk of freezer burn from the cold — or whole, which meant that you needed time to thaw it before use. The best thing, everyone agreed, was to eat it on the same day. Hence the queues outside French bakeries.

She remembered the breadcrumbs on Derek's pullover. Was it such an outlandish idea to try to kill someone with a stale or frozen baguette? She imagined the look on his face as he turned from the piano to face his attacker. Maybe he'd been crushed by the blow before he had a chance to react. The disturbing thought made her shiver and reminded her of the poor man who had drowned in her fishpond the previous year.

At that moment, her phone rang. It wasn't Philippe announcing he'd be late, but Meredith.

"What's up?" Jennifer asked.

"It's that woman," Meredith began. "She's back and she's already stirring the pot!"

"What woman?"

"Sylvie, of course."

"Oh. Well you did know she was going to come back to work at some point . . ."

"Yes," Meredith replied. "But I'd hoped that in her more fragile health, she might be less toxic than before. But it's the opposite. Last night she was laying it on with a trowel, so that we could all see that she thinks she's running the place, and even accused Pippa of being a police informer!"

"She said that at the council meeting? That's slander!" said Jennifer.

"No. Afterwards. And that cow Christine was standing next to her smirking. But the thing is . . ."

"What?"

"Should I tell Pippa?"

Jennifer didn't answer straight away. What was the point of upsetting Pippa unnecessarily? She didn't know how she'd react. What if she marched straight to the *mairie* to confront Sylvie? It risked making things worse. Who would want that woman as an enemy? On the other hand, now that vile rumours were circulating, Pippa had a problem.

"Let me think about it, Meredith," she said, ringing off. She checked the time on her phone. Philippe was due any minute.

CHAPTER 14

That same evening, Pippa sat at Yann's kitchen table armed with a hammer to pull apart a fresh crab.

"I love these *tourteaux*," she said, eyeing the claw that she would leave until last. "There's more flesh on them than other crabs."

"Yes, but unfortunately there are fewer and fewer of them each year," said Yann. He sipped his white wine and refilled her glass. "They say it's a virus."

Pippa had removed the gills and tossed them into an empty dish in front of them. She pulled off the legs and began exploring the white flakes inside with a knife before sucking them clean.

Yann was already smashing his claw gently with the hammer. He did the same with her shell after she nodded encouragement.

"This is delicious," she murmured. They dipped the flesh into Yann's homemade mayonnaise.

"So what's happening?" he asked her as they finished the operation, the crab's shattered remains piled in the dish.

"I was going to ask you," she said. "I can't stop thinking about Tristan accusing me of sabotaging his bakery."

Yann laughed. "I don't think you need to worry about him," he said. "He's not been in touch with us."

Pippa frowned. "What does that mean?"

"If you ask me, maybe he realised that it wasn't sabotage after all," said Yann. "But if he lashed out at you, he's obviously not your friend."

"That's the point," said Pippa. "He's my rival."

Yann got up to wash his hands, then returned to the table where he stood behind her massaging her shoulders.

"Yes he is. But Peeper, there's no need to be paranoid. You thought that you were going to be charged with your friend's murder, remember?"

She looked up at him and laughed, somewhat nervously. Maybe she was becoming paranoid. But there was a reason for it, wasn't there?

"Are you any closer to finding who killed Derek, if it wasn't me?" she asked him, getting up in turn to wash her hands at the sink. Yann picked up the dirty plates and followed her. He took a plate of goat's cheese and Comté from the counter and placed it on the table before responding.

"I can't say that we are," he said. "Solenn came in to talk to us, but she said that she and her husband were very discreet about their lovers."

"You mean they didn't tell each other?"

"Precisely," he said.

"Is that a French thing then?" Pippa wanted to know. Yann laughed.

"You mean having lovers, or not talking about it?"

"You know what I mean," she said. For a moment she scrutinised his face. Was he laughing at her because he was seeing someone else without telling her? But she pushed the thought aside. It was bad enough worrying about Tristan. What if he decided to take his grievances out on her without filing a complaint? She wondered whether to mention her fears to Yann before thinking better of it.

"What if it was one of her lovers who killed Derek?" she asked. "Did you ask her for their identities?"

She could tell from Yann's expression that he didn't like being told how to do his job. And she also knew this was none of her business.

"Never mind," she said, quickly.

Yann clearly wanted to tell her more. "We also asked Solenn about the transactions mentioned in her husband's diary."

"Yes?"

He made a dismissive hand gesture. "It seems that Derek made a generous donation to Médecins Sans Frontières every year on his birthday. According to his wife, it was simply a reminder to himself, as he died only days before his sixtieth birthday."

"Oh." That was disappointing. But Pippa noticed the expression on Yann's face had changed. He lowered his voice and said, "But we think that Derek did know his killer. It's possible that he was expecting this person, which is why he left the back doors open. His fitness clients came in through the garden, didn't they? And there's been an important development in the case."

Pippa held her breath. Yann went on, "You'll find out soon enough because there's going to be an announcement, but I'm telling you this in confidence."

Pippa waited, on the edge of her seat.

"Our forensics say that Derek's injuries were consistent with being struck by a metal or steel rod, like the stick of a golf club."

"Oh dear. Derek used to play golf . . . could it have been one of his partners?"

"We can't rule it out of course. But we found such a weapon in the stream at the bottom of the garden. A rod had been pushed into a baguette, which unfortunately had been mostly eaten by fish before it was discovered. You may remember the breadcrumbs from the murder scene . . ."

"Of course I do. And so you think that was the murder weapon?" Pippa asked. "That's kind of ingenious, using a baguette as disguise."

"Yes, and we do believe it was the weapon. A baguette *magique*," he said, waving one hand in the air. She realised he was referring to a magic wand. That's clever, she thought.

"Can you get the DNA? Problem solved!" she said.

He laughed. "Why does everyone think that DNA solves everything?" he said. "You've been watching too many crime dramas on the TV."

"What do you mean?"

"First of all, you might be interested to know that the majority of murders are solved from fingerprints left at the scene, rather than from DNA testing. And I'm sorry but in this case . . ." He gave a shrug, which she took to mean that such a lead was unlikely to work out.

"You see, with DNA, it's not as simple as you think. It costs money to do the testing, and there can be contamination, and mixed results . . . so we limit what we send to the lab." He looked at her as though to say, "*Need I go on?*" Then he added, "And in this case, where is the DNA if the bread is inside the fishes' stomachs?"

Pippa couldn't help smiling. "But at least we know that a baguette was involved after all!" she said. "What sort of pervert would kill someone like that?"

Yann leaned forward, as though fearing they might be overheard.

"We've also found something else from your friend's phone records," he said. "A caller from England spoke to Derek the day before he died. That person was a Victoria Johnson. And those initials match the VJ written in the diary."

CHAPTER 15

Pippa burst out laughing.

Yann looked crestfallen. "What's the matter?" he asked.

"You do know who Victoria Johnson is, don't you?"

He shook his head.

"It's Vicky! Who used to live here, and who went back to England after her husband died."

"Ah, you mean 'Rockface' the rock star? Oh yes, of course. Why didn't I remember that?" he said. "She was introduced to me as Vicky, not Victoria."

"So, honestly, if you think you've found your killer, I'm sure there'll be an innocent explanation for the diary entry," said Pippa, resolving on the spot to give Vicky a call.

"Very well," said Yann. "You may be right. But we are cooperating with British police who will interview Madame Johnson about the case.

"We did think that the bank transfer and VJ might have been connected," he went on, "but that turned out not to be true."

"Did you get anything else from his phone?" Pippa asked.

"Of course we'd hoped to find some clues. For example, there might have been some communication with the murderer before his death, maybe the day before, or on the day.

That's why we are so interested in Madame Johnson and her telephone call the day before he died. But either the murderer is clever and avoided using phone communication, or there was no such communication."

He sighed. "Let's face it, a lot of communication in our village is in person, isn't it? And that's what makes it all the harder for us to make progress."

* * *

Later that night, Pippa was sitting on her bed back home taking off her clothes when she heard a car driving slowly past the house.

It was such a quiet cul de sac that it was unusual to hear any traffic after the evening rush hour. Maybe it was someone who'd missed a turn and who would go to the end of the street before heading back.

She looked at the clock on the bedside table. It was just after ten, and it was time she was in bed. But she grabbed her dressing gown hanging on the bathroom door and went downstairs.

Once in the living room she looked through a crack in the curtains to see who it could be. But as she peeked out, she was blinded by the full beam from a car's headlights shining straight at her. She jumped back, terrified, closing the curtains.

Who could this be? Her first thought was Bucky, wanting to intimidate her after their confrontation. But what if it was someone else? Maybe Derek's murderer?

She could feel her heart throbbing, and tried to calm herself, thinking: *This is paranoia. Get a grip.*

There had to be a logical explanation. She heard the purr of the car driving away. What a pity she hadn't dared look out again to see the make of car or even get its number plate. But why had they turned round in her drive?

Should she tell Yann? It wasn't too late to call him. But she knew he'd probably tease her as he'd already done about her fear of being branded Derek's murderer.

She went back upstairs slowly. She realised that she and Yann had polished off a bottle of wine between them earlier, and that her over-anxious state could be blamed on the alcohol.

She resolved to abstain over the next few days. It clearly wasn't doing her any good. Alcoholism had taken its toll on quite a few of the villagers, including at least one of the Brits she'd known in Louennec during their pantomime days.

But sleep that night didn't come easily. Although she told herself that the car driver must have had a perfectly innocent reason for doing a three-point turn in her drive, the tiny voice in her head refused to be stilled. When the sound of the alarm crashed into her consciousness at 4 a.m., she was already awake.

CHAPTER 16

"Well?" said Meredith, taking out her wallet to pay for her chicken and six eggs the next day at Jennifer's market stall.

"I'm going to tell her," said Jennifer, with a nervous look in Pippa's direction. "Forewarned is forearmed."

"Very good. I think you're right," said Meredith. She placed the produce carefully in her basket and wandered off to buy some cheese from Philippe who had a long line of customers outside his van.

Sales were brisk that morning, and Jennifer hardly had the time to chat. The market was often busier when the sun was shining, as it was that day. Her customers picked up everything from courgettes to apples, as well as every single chicken. Only once did she catch Bucky's eye as she noticed him glowering at Pippa. Apparently their feud was still alive.

She and Pippa headed for the café as usual after packing up, both pleased with their morning's sales. Philippe gave them a wave from his place at the bar where he was enjoying a *ballon* of red wine with Jean-Luc.

The bearded waiter brought over their coffees, which he put down with a flourish along with the bill. Jennifer decided not to beat about the bush.

"I need to warn you about something," she said, leaning close to Pippa on their bench. "I heard on the grapevine that Sylvie at the *mairie* has got it in for you."

Pippa didn't seem disturbed at the news but waited for Jennifer to continue.

"She seems to think that you're a police informant."

"What? . . . She thinks I'm passing on information to Yann?"

Jennifer gave a sigh, "Yes. I suppose so. It's obviously malicious gossip but I thought I'd better tell you."

Pippa sat back, stunned into silence.

"Are you OK?" Jennifer asked, touching her friend's arm.

"Isn't this what we were talking about the other day? They just don't like us, do they!"

"Look, Pippa. The Bretons don't like the French either, do they? What about that graffiti on the bridge over the main road that says *Français go home*? But the point is that Sylvie is a nasty piece of work and nobody in the village likes her. It's got nothing to do with us being Brits," said Jennifer.

"It doesn't help though, does it?" Pippa hissed. "Who told you this? I can tell you that this is the last thing I need at this point, what with all the mud being thrown in my direction."

Jennifer hesitated. She stirred her café crème and took a sip through the milk foam before responding. "It was Meredith. Apparently Sylvie let it slip after a council meeting. She accused you of passing on information from your customers."

Pippa swallowed hard. "But you know I only do that when the police aren't doing their work properly and I hear something of interest! I wouldn't call it informing, would you? God, *informing* makes it sound like collaborators in the war!"

"No, of course I wouldn't," said Jennifer. She was starting to wonder whether she should have kept her mouth shut.

Pippa was staring into the middle distance, chewing her upper lip.

Eventually, she said, "Yann would be mortified."

"You're not going to tell him, are you?"

"No, of course not..." Pippa was adamant. "If he found out he'd probably go round to Sylvie's and kill her."

"Kill her?"

"No. I'm joking." Pippa was still digesting what she'd been told.

Jennifer finished her coffee, then said, "Talking of village politics, what about Bucky?"

Pippa grinned at the nickname. "He's not followed up, according to Yann," she said, before adding, "but he also told me that they've found the murder weapon — a metal rod pushed inside a baguette!"

"Crumbs!" Jennifer deadpanned. "So you might still be the murderer..."

Pippa didn't laugh. "As you said yourself, there are plenty of places in and around Carhaix where you can buy a baguette," she said. "Including in every supermarket."

"It's weird though, don't you think?" said Jennifer. "Why go to all that trouble?"

"I suppose nobody would pay attention to someone with a baguette under their arm round here. I mean, it concealed the murder weapon, didn't it? And after killing Derek, the murderer went back outside and chucked it into the river. Simple!"

"Well, I suppose it was... Sounds brilliant, actually," Jennifer replied. "It's amazing it doesn't happen more often. Although I suppose you need to have a trout stream handy."

"Or a fishpond," Pippa joked, with a meaningful look at Jennifer, who ignored her.

"By the way," Pippa added, "do you happen to have Vicky's phone number in England? I need to get hold of her because Yann told me that she and Derek were in touch just before he died."

"Oh," said Jennifer, taking out her phone. As she scrolled through her contacts, she looked up and said, "You don't think... do you?"

Pippa laughed. "Of course not! But they're still going to interview her."

"I suppose she could have come over with a baguette from Waitrose, and nobody would have noticed," said Jennifer. "And in fact English baguettes weigh a ton, so she wouldn't have even had to stick a metal rod inside it!"

They both giggled. Then Pippa said, "From what Yann told me, unless the killer strikes again, I don't know how they're ever going to find the murderer."

CHAPTER 17

Jennifer was clearing the kitchen table the next morning when she heard the front door slam.

"What's that?" Philippe asked. He was stacking the dishwasher with the breakfast things and the children had gone upstairs.

Jonathan sauntered in. Jennifer had forgotten that he still had a key, and glanced at Philippe to check his reaction.

Jonathan said, "You'll be pleased to hear I've found a flat in Carhaix. So you won't be getting rid of me that fast." He grinned.

Was this supposed to be funny, Jennifer wondered.

"I'm going to check on the animals, *chérie*," Philippe said straight away.

Jonathan must have caught the term of endearment before Philippe went into the hall to put on his wellies, leaving Jennifer and Jonathan alone.

"So where is your new place?" Jennifer asked.

"Just inside the boulevard ring road. It's a small house, with two bedrooms and space for a sofa bed, so I can take the kids. Happy?"

Jennifer was glad he'd found somewhere and would be staying in Carhaix, but why did he always manage to irritate her? Or maybe she shouldn't allow him to press her buttons, she thought, deciding to ignore his tone of voice.

"That's good," she said. "But why did you come all this way to tell me that?"

"You said you wanted to talk to Mariam with me. Well, here I am."

"For goodness' sake, Jonathan, why didn't you let me know?"

"I *am* letting you know. Didn't she mention? I told her the other day when I gave her some maths coaching."

"No she didn't."

Jennifer hesitated before offering Jonathan a cup of tea or coffee, noticing that he'd made himself comfortable at the kitchen table.

"Sure. A quick coffee, thanks."

She poured him a filter coffee with a drop of milk.

"I'm glad you've come, though," she said. "Because after you left the other day, I discovered some drawings by Mariam under her mattress, and guess what? She's an accomplished artist."

"Oh? What was she drawing?"

"Well, the early ones date from the time she was being bullied. It was pretty obvious to me that that's how she dealt with it."

"I thought the school said she was skipping maths and going walkabout."

"Yes, I know. But I mean *dealt with it* psychologically. Because if you recall, she never wanted to talk about it with us. So maybe it was cathartic for her."

Jennifer glanced at Jonathan because she never knew whether he would blow up in situations like this. But he was staring into his coffee as though divining a meaning.

"Well. Good for her," he said, picking up his mug and taking a long swig of coffee.

Jennifer waited for his eyes to return to her.

"But I also wondered whether the drawings meant that she might have been bullied more recently," she said.

Jonathan frowned, but said nothing.

"I mean, I can't say I've noticed anything, she seems to be a pretty normal teenager with friends . . . but who knows?" she said. "I think we should ask her. We're her parents, after all."

"I see," he said. "So you're going to confess to having invaded her privacy and gone snooping in her bedroom?"

She snorted. "I don't see what else we can do. And I can tell her truthfully that it was completely by accident, while doing her job of making the bed, that I found the bag with the drawings inside."

Jonathan stood up. Jennifer knew he hated this sort of conversation, particularly involving his daughter. In the end he said, "OK. If that's what you want. But why not wait until another day, as we never know how she's going to react? I think we've got enough on our plate with her already today, don't you?"

Jennifer had to admit that his approach made sense. He dropped his empty mug in the sink and headed for the stairs. Jennifer caught up with him, saying, "I was just thinking, is it appropriate that you still have a key?"

Before he could answer, she heard Philippe coming in again.

"We're going to have a chat with Mariam," she explained quickly before following Jonathan up the stairs. They knocked on Mariam's door after Jonathan greeted Luke in his bedroom with a jovial wave. But an expression of barely concealed alarm crossed their daughter's face when she saw the two of them. She turned her chair to face her parents, who sat next to each other on the bed.

"Mariam, we want to talk to you about your birth mother," Jennifer began. "The truth is that we really don't know how to go about finding her, because I'm afraid we don't even have her identity."

"What do you mean? Somebody must know. There must be records somewhere," Mariam snapped.

Jonathan stepped in to say, "Mum means that the adoption agency in London couldn't identify the parents. As we told you, your birth mother was a Somali but because of the war there she ended up across the border in a huge refugee camp in Kenya. And that's where you were found."

"But they'd have records there, wouldn't they? I can write to them! This is ridiculous!" she protested.

Jonathan glanced across at Jennifer, who gave the slightest shake of her head. He said, "Well, although the refugee camp is in Kenya, the thing is, the orphanage found you outside the camp. So that's why we don't know who your birth mother is. Or your birth father, for that matter. All we know is that you were born in Somalia."

Or at least we think you were, Jennifer thought. What if she'd been born in the refugee camp? She tried to look on the bright side. "Let's face it, you could be a Somali princess, for all we know," she said. "You know that you're our princess anyway, don't you?"

Mariam still wasn't thrown off course. Jennifer feared that Jonathan might have given just enough away for Mariam to launch her own investigation.

"OK, so if I was outside the camp, where was I? Surely the orphanage would have a record," Mariam insisted.

"Look, you weren't in the camp, that's what I'm telling you," Jonathan said, a tinge of irritation in his voice. "And I don't know how, so many years later, any of us can find out more."

"But what about DNA? I could get a test!"

Jonathan replied, "And then what? That's all very well, but are you expecting us to get a match by testing random Somalis? Talk about a needle in a haystack!"

Jennifer cringed. She got up to give Mariam a hug, but her daughter turned away. Jennifer still clasped her round the shoulders, moved away a tress of silky black hair and kissed her on the cheek. When she turned round to look at Jonathan, he was standing up to go.

"That's not the end of it, you know," she said in a low voice, behind him in the corridor.

"OK, if you say so," he replied. "But to be honest I don't know what else we can do. There's no point going back to the adoption agency in London after so long as they won't have any more information."

"Let me think about it," Jennifer replied. "Oh, by the way," she added. "Pippa and I were talking about the investigation into Derek's murder with Solenn. I suppose they called you in to make a statement, did they?"

"Oh yes," he replied, stopping dead. "They wanted to know if he had any enemies, that sort of thing."

"And did he? He always seemed very even tempered — classic doctor's bedside manner. But you probably knew him better than me."

"He was certainly fed up with his fitness clients, always complaining about them being lazy sods who didn't pay their subs on time."

"Well it doesn't seem like some lazy sod would have found a reason for smashing his head in, does it? What about his womanising?" Jennifer asked.

Jonathan was so startled he almost jumped. He frowned and said, "What are you talking about?"

"It seems to be common knowledge in the village. Hadn't you heard that he and Solenn had an open marriage?"

Jonathan laughed, clearly embarrassed. Jennifer wondered whether he was thinking about how he'd betrayed her by dating Emma. She remembered that Derek had known all about Jonathan's little lies.

"Oh that!" he replied. "Yes. The cops didn't ask me about that, and I didn't mention it either. Why? Do you think it might be relevant?"

"Yes, because a crime of passion is one of the reasons why murder is committed," she said pointedly. "Did you know who he was screwing?"

Jonathan began walking down the stairs. He said over his shoulder, almost casually, "I don't know whether Derek mentioned all his girlfriends to me, but I do remember hearing about a couple of them. There was a hairdresser from Carhaix, and another woman from somewhere outside Louennec, as far as I can remember. Maybe Kerivac, but I'm not even sure he told me."

"No names? Anyone else? And what about Solenn's boyfriends?"

"What is this?" Jonathan said, reaching the bottom of the stairs. "The Spanish inquisition? Look, I need to get home."

"Don't forget to leave your key," she called out as he turned towards the front door. He put his hand in a trouser pocket and hung the key on the wall before leaving the house without another word.

CHAPTER 18

Pippa recognised the woman behind the bakery counter immediately.

She'd left Gwen in charge under the pretext of having an urgent errand, before driving to the nearby village of Ploumenel. As soon as she pushed open the door, triggering a bell sound, she recognised the blonde with rosebud lips whom she'd seen on the day of Derek's funeral.

"Is your husband in?" Pippa asked, gesturing towards the back room where she suspected Bucky would be at work on a Tuesday morning.

"Qui le demande?" the woman asked.

"My name is Pippa. I'm the baker in Louennec, and I need to see Tristan," she replied.

"Oh yes, of course. I'm Madeleine. I remember you from the market. And the funeral." She smiled pleasantly before flipping up the counter so that Pippa could walk through.

Bucky was bent over a tray of baguettes, which he was about to put in the oven. His face darkened when he looked over his shoulder and saw Pippa.

"Un moment," he said. He placed the baguettes with another batch already cooking inside, then turned round to face her, folding his arms.

"*Bonjour*, Tristan," she began. "I've come to see you because I feel that you owe me an apology."

"An apology?" His voice dripped sarcasm.

"Yes. You may remember that the last time I saw you at the market, in front of all my customers, you accused me of sabotaging your bakery and threatened to file a complaint. Well, I can tell you, I'm still waiting!" she said. She wasn't going to be intimidated by this man.

He screwed up his nose, revealing his prominent upper teeth, which jutted out like a weapon. He was the same height as Pippa and he remained standing, arms folded.

"Ah. That," he said, as though he'd already forgotten. "My apprentice pulled out the wrong plug when he left in the evening."

"*Vous vous foutez de moi?*" Pippa raised her voice but she didn't care that Madeleine might be listening on the other side of the door. "You've got to be kidding! Like I said, Tristan, you owe me an apology. I've not been able to sleep since you levelled your completely unfounded accusations against me."

She took a breath before continuing, "What am I going to do about the reputational damage? I'm the one who should be suing you! What about my customers who heard you shouting at me? What do you suppose they thought? They don't know that your electricity cut had nothing to do with me. And from what you're saying it wasn't even sabotage at all!"

A vein on Bucky's forehead was pulsating. His deep-set eyes shot daggers at her. Pippa thought that if she had a cream puff within reach she'd shove it in his face. He retorted, "Who do you foreigners think you are? You come over here with your fancy ways, you set up in competition to us and what are we supposed to do? I've lost customers because of you!"

"Really?" Pippa replied. "But that's no reason to accuse me of doing things I never did, is it? And as far as competition is concerned, there's enough room in our two villages for more than one bakery. If people come to Louennec to buy my *tropéziennes*, it's because you don't bake them. But that's not my problem, it's yours!"

She'd said her piece. She turned on her heel before walking past Madeleine, who was serving two astonished customers who'd obviously heard everything. *Good*, she thought.

"*Au revoir*," she said over her shoulder, and flounced out to her car.

CHAPTER 19

Pippa sat in the car for a few minutes, still fuming, before setting off for her bakery.

Had she made things worse by confronting Tristan? He must have felt ashamed after accusing her of something caused by his own employee's incompetence. She knew they needed to bury the hatchet before their feud intensified. But how?

She drove past fields of winter wheat on her way back to Louennec, and pulled into the car park next to the *mairie*, where she bumped into Meredith heading in the direction of the bar-tabac.

"Morning," Meredith called out. "Do you want to join me for a quick coffee?"

"Sorry." Pippa gestured towards the bakery. "I'm in a bit of a hurry."

"Oh, by the way," said Meredith, approaching her. "The old lady who lives in that house—" she pointed in the direction of the white fence — "has just died. Madame Briand. You knew her, didn't you?"

"Yes, she was one of my regular customers, although one of her neighbours told me she'd had a fall and so sometimes she'd send her Portuguese carer over. That's sad news."

"Yes, I suppose she must have been getting frail. I hadn't seen her for ages. Did she have all her marbles?"

"Oh yes. She was in her eighties, wasn't she?" Pippa asked.

"She was ninety-one, in fact. Do you remember, she was in a nasty family dispute over the property succession some time ago?"

Pippa nodded. "Yes I do. Awful. She'd always seemed vulnerable to me. Particularly with all that trouble she had after her husband died." She paused. "When did she die, Meredith?"

"Yesterday."

"That's weird," said Pippa. "She came in yesterday morning for a demi-baguette. She was on her own, impeccably dressed as usual, and we had a little chat. She told me she'd had a nasty tummy upset the night before but that she was feeling better. Then she toddled off. I wonder what happened?"

"I don't think there was anything suspicious, if that's what you mean," said Meredith. "Old lady dies, nothing to see here."

The two friends said goodbye. Pippa found Gwen behind the counter at the bakery, serving croissants to a young woman of about the same age. The two of them were deep in conversation, which stopped as soon as she entered.

"*Bonjour*," she said to them. "Everything OK?"

"*Bonjour*, Peeper," said Gwen. "We were just talking about my brother who's been elected first deputy to the mayor. This is my friend Emilie who works with him at the village school."

Emilie smiled.

"So he'll be replacing Jean-Michel — that's great," said Pippa.

Gwen flushed with pleasure. "Thank you. But Erwan says he feels terrible because he was in a competition with someone else and he only won by one vote. So now he knows that half of the council voted against him."

"Oh, I see. Do you know who his competitor was?"

"It was an old guy. I don't know who."

"Well, whoever it was, the main thing is that Erwan got elected. I think the council could do with some younger people," said Pippa.

Gwen didn't respond straight away. When she did, it sounded to Pippa like a warning. "Don't you know what it's like round here? You never know what can happen, with all the family vendettas in this village."

Pippa checked the time, then fished out her phone and gestured that she was stepping outside to make a call. It seemed like a good time to get hold of Vicky. They'd hardly spoken since her return to London some months ago.

She recognised Vicky's harsh east London accent straight away, and smiled at being called "darlin'".

"What's up?" Vicky asked. "I thought you were all ignoring me!"

"No, no, not at all," said Pippa. "But there's been a lot going on. I don't know whether you heard that Derek died about a month ago?" She cleared her throat. "He was murdered."

"Murdered? What the fuck? I spoke to him quite recently, let's see, it was about that time . . . If I'd have known, I'd have come to the funeral."

"I'm sorry. We should have told you."

Pippa waited until Vicky volunteered why the two of them had been in touch. It only took a moment.

"You know what? I'd asked him if he wanted to buy one of Alex's bikes. I've still got a couple of them, and I knew Derek liked bikes. Alex had a Beemer, and I offered it to Derek, but he wasn't sure when we were chatting . . . and he never called me back to confirm. I did think that was a bit strange. He never struck me as the ungrateful type."

"Well, you remember my gendarme friend Yann?"

"Oh yeah, the dish from next door?"

Pippa smiled. "He was the one who told me that your name was in Derek's diary around the time of his death. Maybe Derek had intended to call you back. Please don't say you got this from me, but Yann told me that the police are going to get in contact with you about why you were in touch."

"The police?" Vicky cackled. "Because they think I'm the effing murderer! That's a good one!"

Pippa could imagine the ageing rock chick shaking her henna-dyed hair in disbelief, and smiled.

The two of them said goodbye. But Pippa felt a prick of conscience. What if Yann found out about her tipping off Vicky? Was she influencing the investigation unwittingly?

She'd done it again, she realised. She'd heard confidential information and had interjected herself into a police investigation. But was it fair to accuse her of being a police informer?

And yet . . . it was true that she'd passed on information to Yann in the past, little snippets from her customers that she'd thought would be helpful in an investigation. And they had been. Yann had even thanked her. But it was quite another thing to accuse her of being an informant. She wouldn't put it past Sylvie to have invented the baseless accusation to see whether the mud would stick.

Then she remembered her conversation with Yann during which he'd confided to her about how Solenn had admitted to keeping her sex life secret from Derek and vice versa. But the whole village already knew about her and Derek having an open marriage, didn't they? Maybe he shouldn't have mentioned her admission; such information would be covered by what the French called the *secret de l'instruction*. But what was she supposed to talk about with her gendarme boyfriend? And he knew he could trust her discretion. Or could he?

Pippa was struck with remorse as she remembered the occasions when she'd passed on information to Jennifer that Yann had given her with the explicit instruction of keeping it to herself. Most recently when he'd confided in her before the official announcement about Derek having been fatally wounded by a metal rod inside a baguette. She resolved that in future, she would respect the confidentiality he requested. It was the least she could do, in the light of Sylvie's insinuations.

CHAPTER 20

"Just the three of us, that's nice," said Jennifer.

Solenn smiled as she finished pouring Jennifer and Pippa a glass of wine.

"Is Meredith coming?" Pippa asked.

"I did invite her, but she's seeing her daughter tonight," said Solenn. Pippa glanced across at Jennifer at the unspoken reference to Emma, but her friend was staring at the garden through the bi-fold windows.

Solenn, dressed in a pencil skirt and her usual heels while her English guests were in comfortable jeans and baggy tops, ushered them towards the long dining table set for three. It was hard to ignore the piano beside the wall. It was a smart black upright with a high gloss finish. Its lid was down. Pippa wondered how Solenn coped with the memory.

"Now," Solenn said, injecting a cheerful note into the proceedings. "Sit yourselves down. I've made roast chicken and as it's one of Jennifer's I'm sure it will be super delicious."

The other two smiled, and offered to help, but Solenn insisted that she could manage. She disappeared for a few moments before returning with the dinner plates which she placed on the table. Pippa reached out to touch hers. Jennifer caught her eye and winked. They'd both noticed that the plates were cold, in true French tradition.

Solenn came out again with the chicken, which she'd already cut into rough pieces on another cold plate. She then brought out a jug of sauce and some green beans. The French would never adopt the meat and two veg diet, Pippa thought.

"Did you hear that the brother of my apprentice, Gwen, is going to be the new first deputy to Meredith?" Pippa said once they'd all served themselves. "Apparently he's not that happy about it."

"Why's that?" Solenn asked.

"I don't know. The result was seven votes to eight for Erwan. Gwen seemed to think there might be problems."

"*Pff*, problems," said Solenn. "So many petty rivalries in our *commune*," she said.

"You mean political disputes?"

She shook her head. "Oh no. Not in an election like that. Most of the councillors don't have a political affiliation, although we know exactly who thinks what," she said, narrowing her eyes. "It's more likely to be family stuff. Goes back generations."

Jennifer leaned forward. "And so do you know who might have wanted to stop Gwen's brother?"

Solenn looked at the ceiling while she finished a morsel of chicken, then replied, "Sylvie, I imagine. Because she hates everyone, doesn't she? And if she thought Meredith supported one candidate, that would be enough for her to support another."

"So true," said Pippa. They finished their dish and wiped the plates with some torn baguette, ready for the cheese course.

"Solenn, do you think it might be a feud like that which led to Derek's murder?" Pippa asked tentatively.

Solenn gave a doubtful pout. "I wouldn't know, but I don't think so. Would you believe it, the investigators asked me about our love life!" She sat up, as though preening herself on the compliment.

"Really?" said Pippa. "I wonder why . . ."

"Well someone must have told them we had a *mariage libre*," she said. "But the point of that was that neither Derek nor I knew about the other's lovers. Those were the rules."

"But what about trust?" said Jennifer. "How could that work? And what if one of the people got hurt? And didn't you get jealous?"

"It's only sex," said Solenn, puzzled by Jennifer's apparent prudishness. "I mean, we weren't going to leave each other. And our marriage remained fresh."

"OK, well," said Pippa. "Whatever floats your boat," she added in English.

"*Exactement*," Solenn replied, crossing and uncrossing her perfectly shaped legs like Sharon Stone in *Basic Instinct*. She got up and brought in a plate of cheeses which she said she'd bought from Philippe.

"But wait a minute," said Jennifer. "The only reason the police would be asking you about your love life is if they think that one of your lovers might have a reason for killing Derek."

"Of course," said Solenn. "And it's their job to find them, isn't it? Not mine. It would be too distressing for me to ask a lover if they'd betrayed me or Derek."

Really? Pippa couldn't help thinking, *Does Solenn want her husband's murder to be solved or not?*

"Have you heard anything from the investigation? They must be interviewing other people too," Jennifer asked Solenn.

"Yes of course they are conducting interviews, but I haven't heard anything specific from the police. Have you, Peeper?"

Pippa shook her head, embarrassed at Solenn assuming she might be in the loop. She picked up the cheese knife and helped herself to a slice of perfectly ripe Brie.

"I'm sure they've contacted Derek's golfing friends, and his clients. He was always complaining about his fitness classes and that's why he wanted to stop work. You might have seen some of his clients at the funeral . . ." Solenn went on.

Jennifer and Pippa looked at each other.

"Yes, but do you think the murderer would have shown up at the funeral?" Jennifer asked.

"Why not?" Solenn replied. "Do help yourselves to cheese. The Saint-Nectaire is delicious."

CHAPTER 21

Pippa was about to close the bakery when she noticed a young couple pointing at cakes in the window.

It was at that time of day when people on their way home from work usually came in to buy reduced price items which she sold through an app. It didn't bring in much, but at least the food wouldn't go to waste.

The pair came in and asked for her lucky dip. When they pointed towards the window display, she had to explain that what she dropped into the bag was her choice, not theirs. Sometimes customers got pushy but these two paid for the croissants and apple turnovers in their brown bag without demur and left.

The sun was setting when she walked home from the shop. She'd taken to wearing a jacket because of the October nip in the air.

As she approached her house she heard a car behind her. Yann lowered the driver's window and gave her a wave as he pulled into his drive.

"Ca *va?*" he asked.

"Ca *va,*" she replied, waiting for him on her side of the low box hedge that demarcated their properties.

"Anything new?" she asked warily, as he got out of his car.

"You mean on the investigation?" he said. "Not much."

"So no breakthrough yet, then?"

Yann shook his head in reply. Pippa felt embarrassed, remembering her visit to Tristan's bakery.

"Hmm. Yes, I see," she said. "Are you still free on Saturday?"

"Of course, Peeper," he said with a smile. "*Bonne soirée.*"

She left him taking things out of the boot and opened her front door. As she bent down to pick up an envelope on which her address was written in spidery handwriting, her phone rang. She kicked the door shut with one foot and answered. It was Jennifer.

"Look, do you mind if I pick your brains about the drawings I found under Mariam's mattress? I think you might be able to help," she said.

Pippa frowned, worrying about her own time constraints, but understood that Jennifer must have been thinking about how to move forward with Mariam ever since her discovery.

"Yes . . . ?" she said, somewhat hesitantly.

"I'm wondering about maybe talking to Jonathan about paying for private classes for her because she's only getting an hour a week at school. She's good."

Pippa was relieved. Maybe all her friend was after was a little reassurance.

"She obviously didn't want me to know, though," Jennifer went on. "That's why she didn't leave them lying around but went to the trouble of hiding them under the mattress. Weirdly, when I asked her recently what she wanted to do in life, she said she wanted to be an artist!"

"That's interesting. And to me it shows how resilient she is. I mean, she drew her way out of a difficult time."

"Yes. I'm ringing though because I was wondering if you'd take a look."

"I can't teach her, if that's what you mean. I wouldn't have time. And is it a good idea? I can't see how I can ask her out of the blue. But I'd be happy to help in some way."

"Thank you," said Jennifer. "I agree that first of all I'll have to come clean with her about having found them. Then maybe we could engineer a conversation with you. And based on what you think about her talent, I'll try to persuade Jonathan and we'll find an art teacher."

Pippa agreed with the plan and rang off, taking the post into the kitchen.

She examined the envelope with its strange handwriting. She'd never received a letter like this before. There was no sender's address and it had been hand-delivered.

She slit the envelope open and took out the single paper sheet inside. As she realised what it was, she gasped, dropping the letter onto the kitchen table. The sender had gone to the trouble of cutting out letters from a newspaper or magazine and pasting them onto the sheet. There was no signature.

The message, in French, read: *"Félicitations pour la mort de Mme Briand, tué*e par vos baguettes" — Congratulations on the death of Mme Briand, killed by your baguettes.

CHAPTER 22

Pippa burst into tears and sat down heavily on a chair.

The absence of a stamp on the envelope obviously meant that it was from somebody who had dropped it off at the house, somebody from Louennec or nearby, she presumed.

She studied the letters pasted onto the page again. Who could have gone to such trouble to accuse her of killing one of her customers in an anonymous letter? And why?

Casting around in her memory, she wondered whether there might be any connection with Derek's death. Or could it be Tristan, who had raised their feud to a new level, just when she wanted to dial it down?

She got up, still clasping the letter, and without picking up her jacket she went round to Yann's.

He opened the door straight away, and led her inside by the hand, noticing the tears running down her face.

"What's the matter?"

She held out the letter. "Look at this," she mumbled.

"Come in," he said, taking it. They went into his kitchen and sat on stools beside each other at the counter.

"*Un corbeau*," he said, frowning. She looked blank. Why was he talking about a crow? Noticing her reaction, he added, "It's a poison pen letter. That's what we call them in French.

I'm afraid it's not terribly unusual in rural areas; you know how disputes can escalate round here."

"But look what it says — I'm being accused of having murdered Madame Briand!"

Yann laid a comforting arm round her shoulder, and drew her to him.

"I can see that. Leave this with me, Peeper. The *mairie* should have the old lady's death certificate. We'll take it from there. But it could be that we might have to open an investigation, in the light of this."

Pippa could feel her cheeks wet with tears. "But shouldn't you be taking this poison pen letter seriously? It's obviously malicious! How could any of my baguettes have killed anybody? Somebody is trying to pin the blame on me."

Yann got up in search of paper tissues and wiped her tears.

"I'm just saying that we can investigate. But that's not my decision. Don't worry, Peeper, everything will be alright. I'm not suggesting you murdered an old lady."

She shot him a surprised look, as though he'd already abandoned her by even contemplating that she might have.

"Did this letter come in an envelope?" he went on.

"Yes. I left it at home. It had handwriting on the front. And no stamp, so the culprit must be local."

"OK. Show me. The handwriting was probably disguised, of course," he said.

"But I want to know how I should react to this. Should I file a complaint with the gendarmerie? Can they check the CCTV?"

"*Tu rigoles*," he said. But she wasn't joking. "We're not in London here, as you might have noticed," he said. "We don't have cameras on every lamp post like you do."

"I'm just saying that somebody may have recognised the culprit posting the letter through my door, if it was in the daytime. What about those video doorbells? Maybe someone in our cul de sac . . . ?"

"What about, what about . . ." he repeated. "Peeper, I have already told you, let us do the investigation. Don't you trust us?"

"Yes of course I do." She felt sheepish, but why couldn't she be involved in solving a crime that had targeted her?

"Though you could try to find a graphologist who might be able to help with identifying the writer. Is there anyone you suspect?" Yann asked.

"Look, this has only just happened. But I can't really think of anyone in the village who hates me that badly. The only person I don't have good relations with is Tristan, the guy I told you about who accused me of sabotaging his bakery."

Yann was stroking his chin. "Oh yes. The one who didn't contact us."

"Yes. Quite. Do you think he might be behind it?"

As usual, Yann avoided committing himself. "Maybe, maybe not," he said. "Don't worry. We'll get to the bottom of this. But first you must file a complaint."

CHAPTER 23

"It's Daddy!" Luke yelled, triggering a loud bark from Byron.

Luke ran downstairs, followed by Mariam, who was curious to see what was going on.

Jennifer went to the front door to let Jonathan in. "Hello, little fella," he said to Luke. "You ready to help?"

Jennifer had been expecting Jonathan to clear out his remaining things to take to his new house, and had decided to let him and the children get on with it that evening. She somehow felt that it wasn't appropriate for her to join in, and in any case Philippe was finishing his ice cream in the kitchen. But she'd excused herself from the table, saying she'd just lend a hand taking things down from the loft.

"Shall we go up there?" said Jonathan at the bottom of the stairs.

Even Mariam was curious, and she trailed behind them. Jonathan pulled down the ladder to the loft and switched on a light inside.

"Either of you coming up?" he asked. "If you've finished your homework, that is."

Mariam pulled a face and said something about spiders, but Luke was already climbing the ladder to survey the loft's contents from the top.

"There's lots of boxes up here," he said. "You're not taking all of them, are you?"

"I've marked the ones I need with my name," Jonathan said. "You can keep the surfboard."

Luke frowned. "I didn't even know we had one!" he said.

"Come down, Luke," said Jennifer. "They're going to be too heavy for you to manage. Let me help Daddy."

Mariam had returned to her room. Jonathan passed down six or seven boxes to Jennifer, who struggled to carry them down the ladder before dropping them onto the corridor floor.

"Are you going to be able to take them all in one go?" she asked.

"I'll probably need to make two journeys. But that will be it," he said. Jennifer realised that this was a big moment. Jonathan moving into a separate house by himself was definitely it. There was no going back. She felt a wave of sadness envelop her. But she knew she mustn't let it show. The main thing was to make sure that the children were on board, she thought.

She knocked on Mariam's door and went inside. Mariam turned round and took out her earbuds.

"Are you going to see Daddy's new house? I think it would be a good idea. You can bag your room before Luke does."

Mariam smiled. "Yes. OK. In a minute."

Jennifer swallowed, seeing her chance.

"Is everything OK at school?"

Mariam seemed genuinely taken aback by the question. "Why?"

"Well, I should tell you that I know about your drawings. I'm sorry, I found them by accident when I was making your bed a little while ago. They're really good."

Mariam still looked perplexed.

Jennifer stumbled on. "I mean, there's one in particular that seemed to show that girl hurting you in the playground. Maeli. I was just wondering whether you've been bullied again more recently?" she said gently.

Mariam shook her head vigorously, then raised her eyes to heaven.

"No," she said. "Don't worry, everything's fine."

"That's good. That's what I thought," Jennifer murmured as Mariam got up and left the room.

She watched Mariam feel round the rim of the boxes to test their weight. Then her daughter looked up at Jonathan, who was peering down from the attic.

"Can I take this one down to the car?" she said.

"Sure," he said. "Are you coming with us?"

"Yeah."

"Luke? Come on, we need some help here," Jonathan called out. Luke appeared from his bedroom and picked up a small box.

"What's in this one?" he asked. "It's heavy."

"What does it say? Oh. Books. Take another one with clothes, that'll be easier."

The two children made their way downstairs to the car. Jonathan turned to Jennifer and said, "I've already bought some new cutlery and plates."

"What about white goods?" she asked. When he'd moved in to Emma's place he'd only taken a suitcase or two of clothes, just the bare minimum.

"No need, thank God," he said. "The kitchen's fully equipped. The house is modern, it was only built a few years ago."

"Oh. Great."

She felt awkward. Here they were making small talk but she didn't know what to say.

"I'd better go down," she said, motioning with one hand.

"Of course. The three of us can manage this."

She turned away, then looked back at him.

"So does this mean you're staying?" she asked.

Jonathan looked puzzled.

"I mean, staying in France. You're not going back to England?"

He raised his hand to his forehead to brush away sweat, then smiled.

"No. I'm staying."

"That's good," she said, before adding, "By the way, I've just had a little chat with Mariam about the bullying. She says everything's fine."

"So now we can all relax," he said.

"I also told her about how I found the drawings. At least she didn't go off the deep end, but I think it would be nice to encourage her, don't you?"

He looked at her warily.

"What if I find her a private teacher? I think it would do her good," she said.

Jonathan hesitated for a moment. "Sure. Why not?" he said, to her surprise.

CHAPTER 24

As soon as the house fell silent, Jennifer installed her laptop on the dining room table, with Byron at her feet.

"At last, some peace and quiet," she said to him, nudging the dog with her slippered foot. He rolled over, paws in the air, expecting a tummy rub, which she gave him.

She started googling Kenyan refugee camps until she found the one she was looking for. She remembered the name Daadab as soon as it came up on her screen. She'd had the impression that the huge camp, first set up in the Somalia civil war, had been closed down some years ago. But there it was: it was now a complex of three camps, which were home to 240,000 refugees, almost all of them Somali.

What's more, she learned that a new mass influx of refugees had entered the camp, fleeing drought and famine in southern Somalia in 2011, the year after Mariam was born. That had to mean that finding her birth mother among so many people, even assuming she'd stayed in the camp, was going to be daunting. Even now, Jennifer read, thousands of Somalis were still streaming into Daadab. She found it hard to imagine that generations of Somalis must be living there now.

What was Mariam's birth mother's story? What hardships had she suffered? Was she even still alive? How many siblings might Mariam have, she wondered. And under what circumstances did she leave Mariam by the side of a road . . . Maybe there were some things it was better not to know, she thought, looking up from her laptop.

She sighed. Jonathan was right, this was going to be like looking for a needle in a haystack. But didn't they owe it to their daughter to exhaust all possible avenues of investigation?

She got up and went into the kitchen to make herself a cup of tea. Byron trailed after her, sinking onto his blanket covered in golden hairs in exhaustion, possibly wondering why she couldn't make up her mind and sit still.

By the time she took her mug of tea back into the dining room, she had a plan. She went back online and searched for a way to contact the camp. She saw that the UN refugee agency was running it with other partners at the invitation of the Kenyan government. There were even resettlement schemes to relocate refugees to third countries.

Reading this, Jennifer's heart was in her mouth. What if . . . ?

But she didn't even know the woman's name. She might have been resettled to anywhere. This was hopeless. She gave another long sigh, causing Byron to look up at her in concern with his beautiful brown eyes.

Then she had another thought. It was obviously a long shot, but as Mariam had wanted to track down her mother, maybe the mother had tried to find out what had happened to her daughter. A message from Jennifer might be the lynchpin that could solve the riddle.

By now, Jennifer was bubbling over with excitement. She had a whole new narrative in which everyone would live happily ever after.

She took down a series of email addresses of agencies that might be concerned, in order to spread her net as wide as possible, and provided as many relevant details as could prove helpful in a search for the birth mother.

Then she composed identical messages to five different addresses, and hit Send.

CHAPTER 25

That Saturday, Pippa watched from behind her market stall as Meredith approached, her hooded eyes fixed on her.

Her gypsy skirt swayed in time with her deliberate gait. She came to a halt in front of Pippa and said loudly, "There was some excitement at the *mairie* this week. A gendarme came in looking for Madame Briand's death certificate and told Sylvie that you'd received a poison pen letter!"

"Oh no! Why did he have to tell her?" Pippa said in a low voice, frowning at Meredith. She looked around, fearful that they might be overheard in the crowded market.

"He obviously had to explain why he needed the certificate. And she obviously knows we're friends and just happened to mention . . ."

"God, that woman!" Pippa exploded. "Why does she hate me so much?"

Her eyes slid across the market and she could see Bucky watching them.

"I don't think it's you in particular," said Meredith. "It's all of us, probably. She's just a sick person, I'm afraid. I try to ignore her as much as possible these days. But what's this about your anonymous letter?"

Pippa lowered her voice further to avoid being overheard. "Yann thought I could try a graphologist in case they could identify the suspect from the handwriting on the envelope," she concluded.

Meredith looked dubious. "You could try, I suppose," she said. "But when I got a death threat on the *mairie* website, the police never managed to track down the sender. Anyway, I was told that Madame Briand died of natural causes. Why on earth would someone accuse you and your baguettes?"

"Beats me," said Pippa. "But who would know more? The old woman didn't have any family in the village, did she?"

She noticed some customers peering round Meredith and added, "Sorry, look, there are people behind you . . ."

Meredith shifted sideways so that a young couple could step to the front and check out Pippa's display. But before she left, she said, "There's one person in the village who'd know all the details, because she makes it her business."

Pippa frowned and said, "You mean . . . ?"

"Yes. Sylvie Le Goff."

* * *

The Central Café was busy when Pippa and Jennifer arrived for their weekly coffee.

As soon as the waiter took their order, Jennifer said, "What's going on with Meredith? You two were thick as thieves this morning."

"I think Bucky noticed too. Meredith told me that the gendarmerie are investigating the poison pen letter I received, and they went to the *mairie* looking for Madame Briand's death certificate. According to Meredith, she died of natural causes."

"So what's with the poison pen, then?"

Pippa stiffened. The waiter set down their coffees with a glass of water and she took a sip of her café noisette.

"Somebody has it in for me, that's what . . . it's obviously completely made up!" she said. She leaned closer to

Jennifer and added, "The thing is, that ever since I got that letter, every time a customer comes into the bakery, I think it might be them! It's making me completely paranoid."

Jennifer stretched out a hand and patted Pippa's arm. "Chill. It must be someone mentally ill to do a thing like that. But I wonder why you were accused of killing the old lady with your baguettes? And how, exactly? Was she coshed with one, like Derek?"

"That's exactly the point. Meredith said that the only person who'd know about the cause of death would be herself and *la secrétaire de la mairie*. And Meredith just told me it was natural causes."

"Sylvie Le Goff. Of course," said Jennifer. "But what are you going to do about it?"

"Don't worry, I'm working on it," said Pippa with a grin. "But what's happening with you?"

"Oh, just the same old, same old. But I did get some intelligence from Jonathan the other day about Derek's lovers, although he was a bit vague. He said one woman he was seeing was a hairdresser in Carhaix, and another one somewhere outside Louennec, maybe Kerivac. Although of course I don't know whether he was seeing both simultaneously, or even how long ago this was. He might have been quite the Don Juan, for all we know."

"That is vague," said Pippa, grinning. "What are we supposed to do about it?"

"I was just wondering whether you might mention it to Yann. To see whether they know about the hairdresser at least?"

Pippa grimaced. "Look, it's not the best time for me to be interfering in the investigation, is it? I think I may have overstepped the mark by calling Vicky myself. The police are contacting her anyway and I'm sure she'll tell them the same thing that she told me."

They both sat back while they finished their coffees. Jennifer said, "I'm trying to find a moment for bonding with Mariam, so we can talk about her artwork and maybe get her to show you. We might take a trip to the coast, just the two of us. Philippe says he'd look after Luke, the two of them get on really well."

"You really struck gold with him," said Pippa, looking across to the bar where Philippe was chatting with his friend Jean-Luc over a *ballon de rouge*. She looked for her wallet and called the waiter over to pay the bill. "I'd better get back to the bakery."

"And I'll see if I can pull you-know-who away from the bar," said Jennifer, slipping on her jacket.

Pippa strolled towards her car which was parked nearby. Her phone rang and she took it out of her jacket pocket to answer. The caller had an unknown ID.

A male voice identified himself as a reporter with *Le Télégramme*. Pippa's heart began to race. She had a bad feeling before he even spoke.

"How can I help?" she asked.

"I'm ringing about *le corbeau*," the caller replied.

CHAPTER 26

Pippa felt almost queasy when she opened the paper on Monday morning after carrying her morning *café au lait* to the kitchen table.

She scanned the front page nervously, after wiping croissant crumbs from her hand. There was nothing except revolting Breton farmers tipping manure onto the roads and blocking the autoroute with their tractors in their latest conflict with the government. *Nothing new there.*

She flicked through the paper slowly until she reached the page devoted to Louennec. Usually, it contained little other than articles about a local *fest-noz* or a farmer driving into a ditch under the influence, sometimes illustrated with a picture from Jennifer.

But the headline on the top story read: "*Baker files complaint after being accused of baguette murder of villager.*"

Not only that, but the story was alongside a photograph of the letter. Her heart sank. Such bad publicity could ruin her, she thought. What if *le corbeau* was Tristan, her rival? *Cui bono?* But she couldn't accuse him without any proof, like he'd done to her.

She read on. The article quoted her saying how she felt violated. She wished she'd never spoken to that reporter.

Maybe they wouldn't have published the article if she'd refused to speak to him. But she realised that they must have been tipped off by a source in the gendarmerie. Or what if it was someone else? She was sure that Yann would never betray her trust, and in any case he'd told her that he wasn't involved in investigating her complaint.

She put down her coffee cup, thinking that maybe it wasn't such a disaster after all. The article might help the police in solving the crime. But hadn't Meredith told her that was extremely unlikely?

It was already 10 a.m. and Pippa's only day off in the week. She had to go to the bakery in the afternoon to prep for opening on Tuesday morning, but otherwise her day was free.

She went upstairs to put on some make-up, trying to smooth the crease between her eyebrows. Then she went down to the kitchen to wash her breakfast dishes, and took a jacket off the hook before heading round the corner to the *mairie*.

She found Sylvie Le Goff guarding Meredith's office in an anteroom which was at least as big as that of the mayor.

Sylvie looked up from her desk. Pippa couldn't tell whether she was surprised to see her.

"*Oui Madame?*" Pippa noticed she hadn't even bothered with the nicety of saying "*Bonjour.*"

Pippa didn't bother with the niceties either. She flung down *Le Télégramme* onto the desk, open at the Louennec page.

"What is your explanation for this?" she demanded.

Sylvie feigned surprise and pretended to read the news for the first time.

"I'm afraid I can't help you with this matter," she said coldly, pursing her thin lips.

"Someone leaked details of this poison pen letter to the paper," said Pippa. "And I believe that person was you!"

Sylvie stood up, placing both hands on the desk and giving Pippa a death stare from under her painted eyebrows, which were raised in an expression of permanent surprise. For the first time, Pippa took in the full measure of the woman's power.

"You must be aware that Madame Briand died of natural causes, according to her death certificate. So I need to know who is spreading malicious lies about her having been killed by baguettes from my bakery!"

"Ha!" Sylvie replied. "But it is well known in the village that Madame Briand choked to death while eating a baguette. And we all know that she was one of your customers." She crossed herself ostentatiously as though committing Madame Briand to heaven.

"I see," said Pippa, menacingly. "Well, whether you wrote this anonymous letter or not, it's clear that you were at the centre of the libellous gossip that triggered this baseless accusation against me. I was right to have filed a complaint. But what I should have done is filed the complaint against you!"

"I want damage!" Sylvie shouted in English. Pippa almost burst out laughing at the mistake but instead responded by emitting a loud "*pff*" and then saying, also in English, "You've got a fat chance of *damages*." She didn't care whether Sylvie had understood or not.

"Anyway," she said. "It's obvious to me that this letter was specifically designed to undermine my business, if not put me out of work!"

"Madame. Please calm down. You have no proof of anything that you are saying."

Sylvie had recovered her composure and sat down again. She looked across the desk at Pippa as though their conversation was at an end and there was nothing more to be done.

But Pippa was now even more riled. She turned on her heel and stormed out of the building without saying goodbye.

CHAPTER 27

Pippa's blood was still boiling when she decided to drop in on Jennifer that afternoon.

She found her friend at the far end of the smallholding, heaving some extra hay into the sheep pen. She watched as the ewes pushed their faces through the railings, baa-ing with excitement.

"Oi! Take your turn," said Jennifer, throwing a handful of hay in Rambo's direction. She turned as Pippa approached, alerted by a lazy bark from Byron who was sitting by the fishpond.

"I'm finishing up here," she said. "Do you want a cuppa? Come on, Byron." At the mention of his name, he wagged his tail and struggled to his feet.

"Sure. What happened to the lambs?" Pippa asked as they made their way back to the house, the golden retriever trailing behind them.

"They're in the freezer," Jennifer said with a grin. "Don't you remember eating Percy the other day? Mildred is in there as well, now, so he's got company.

"I'm trying to save money," she explained as they headed towards the house. "But that means I need to sell Rambo before he impregnates one of the ewes again. And then I guess I'll get them slaughtered for their meat."

"Oh. You'll miss them, won't you?"

"Yes. Particularly Blackie, the one with the black head. Luke's got really attached to her. But the price of feed and hay is going up, not to mention the vet's fees, etcetera." Jennifer sighed. "I mean, now that Jonathan's gone I'm the only one paying the bills, although he does give me money for the kids, and I can't expect Philippe to chip in, can I?"

The square house, with granite trim round the windows, was starting to show its age. Yellow lichen clung to the slate roof, and the paint on the wooden window frames was peeling. The sight reminded Jennifer of further expenses ahead. She opened the front door, under a twine of wisteria, and took off her wellies. Pippa also removed her shoes, which were slightly muddy from walking along the track.

"I'm feeling the pinch too," said Pippa, pulling a face. "Sometimes I wonder whether I did the right thing moving here."

Jennifer gave her a sharp look. "What's up? That doesn't sound like you," she said.

"I had it out with Madame Le Goff this morning about the poison pen letter," Pippa confessed.

"Really? I don't think I'd dare take on that woman," Jennifer grimaced. "Come through, let's put the kettle on."

Pippa settled in at the kitchen table and watched Jennifer fill the kettle and throw teabags into two mugs.

"Well, I'm glad I did," she said. "She confirmed that the whole thing about me killing Madame Briand was completely made up! The only grain of truth was that the old lady choked to death on a piece of baguette. So all Sylvie had to do was to mention that she bought her baguettes from me, and then died suddenly — Bingo! What an amazing coincidence, eh?"

Jennifer put down their teas on the table. "Oh my God," she said. "So you're saying she's made out that you're guilty by association."

"Yes, and she's trashed my reputation by doing that, now it's all over the newspaper," Pippa said, her voice breaking with emotion.

"What are you talking about?" said Jennifer. "You mean *Le Télégramme?* It must still be in the mailbox. Why didn't you tell me?"

Pippa smiled. "Because I was too upset when I saw it this morning. That's when I summoned up the courage to go round and confront Sylvie directly. I was afraid that Meredith might have heard the commotion from her office, but she never came out, thank goodness."

She added, "I do feel a bit embarrassed about going round there. I mean, I lost my cool. But at least I found out what had happened. I wish I'd known that before I spoke to the reporter who called me."

"Did you tell Yann?" Jennifer asked.

"Not yet, no. But I will," Pippa replied. She took a long sip of tea before continuing. "He told me they might investigate because of what the letter said, and that could be more likely now that journalists have got hold of it. But I hope they won't. I mean, I'm convinced it must have been Sylvie, but I don't have any concrete proof and why draw even more negative attention to me and my bakery through an investigation?"

Jennifer did her best to reassure her friend. Then she carried her empty mug to the sink, picking up Pippa's on her way.

"I've got to pick up the kids," she explained.

"Where's Philippe?" Pippa asked.

"Oh, he's ripening cheese at his place, as usual."

They both walked into the hall and put on their shoes. When Pippa stood up she seemed to crumple. Jennifer put an arm round her shoulder.

"Pippa, don't let this malicious gossip get to you," she said. "You've done nothing wrong and everybody in the village must realise that."

"I hope so," Pippa replied, with a mournful look. "But I worry that this fake news can have consequences in the real world. For me and for my business."

She turned to stare at Jennifer with her eyes wide open.

"Oh my God, I just thought of something," she said. "What about guilt by association? Whoever has sent this anonymous letter could be trying to make a connection between Madame Briand's death and Derek's! And blaming me for both!"

CHAPTER 28

It was Saturday night and Pippa was glad for the chance to forget her cares at a *méchoui* at Daniel Le Floch's farm to which all the locals had been invited.

She sifted through the contents of her wardrobe, wondering what to wear. Although Yann never seemed to mind the way she dressed, she was acutely aware that most of the time she wore a baggy jumper and jeans or leggings under her apron at the bakery.

She pulled out a floral calf-length dress and put it on. Mercifully, it still fitted. Then she did her make-up before setting off.

When Pippa arrived at the farm outside Louennec, the evening was already in full swing. She and Gwen, Daniel's daughter, had prepared piles of bread earlier to accompany the grilled lamb which was turning on a spit outside the barn amid clouds of smoke.

She surveyed the scene of about thirty people, a convivial mix of English and French, where the first group was shouting in order to make themselves understood, and the latter waved their hands around for the same purpose. *This is what I love about living in France*, she thought.

She caught sight of Jennifer and gave her a thumbs up. As she stood by a trestle table to collect a glass of wine, she realised she was standing next to Madeleine from the rival bakery and grimaced with embarrassment. "*Bonsoir*, Peeper," said Madeleine in a friendly way. "I'm sorry you had a misunderstanding with my husband the other day."

Pippa felt mortified, remembering how she'd gone off at the deep end that morning.

"I'm sorry too," she murmured. "Tristan told me that it was his apprentice who'd pulled out an electric plug."

"He should have apologised to you," said Madeleine. "I suggest that we forget about it. Just ignore him — that's what I do!"

Pippa laughed. She and Madeleine were fellow sufferers, working terrible hours in tough conditions. She had an axe to grind with Tristan, not his wife, after all.

"You and I should be swapping recipes," she said.

"I have a nice one for olive bread," said Madeleine. Pippa wondered whether to reciprocate by sharing the recipe for her successful *tropéziennes* cakes. Not likely, she thought.

"I'd love that," she replied. "But I don't want to steal your customers!"

Madeleine smiled. "We're sufficiently far away not to be in competition with each other," she said. "And in any case, we only bake a small number of those loaves.

"Do you know Christine?" Madeleine asked. They'd been joined by a squat woman wearing glasses.

"*Bonsoir*, Christine. Yes of course." Pippa knew perfectly well that this occasional customer of hers was Meredith's toxic deputy, who was close to Sylvie. But could she also be in cahoots with Madeleine?

"How do you two know each other?" Pippa asked, intrigued.

"We're neighbours," said Madeleine. "We've known each other for years, haven't we?"

Christine nodded, leaving Pippa to wonder at the close-knit relationships in the villages of rural France. It always amazed her how everyone knew everyone else — and their private business. But then again, it would be much the same story back in the English countryside . . .

A long-haired violinist at the back of the barn had struck up a Breton dance, and they turned round to watch. Groups of four and two began forming.

"We must find Tristan," said Madeleine. As she and Christine wandered off, Pippa heard cheers outside. She went out and saw villagers applauding Daniel and two of his farm hands, who were heaving the lamb onto a metal table where it was to rest for a while before being carved. Gwen was also busy, setting two long tables with knives and forks for the guests. The evening was mild and the skies were clear for a change.

Pippa returned to the bar and asked for a top-up before going over to Jennifer and Philippe.

"Where's Yann?" Philippe asked.

"He's working, but might come later. What about the children?" Pippa asked Jennifer. "Aren't they here?"

Jennifer laughed. "Are you kidding? Mariam doesn't eat meat, and Luke had other plans, so I've left them at home. They'll be fine."

Somebody slapped Philippe on the shoulder and he turned round. It was his friend Jean-Luc from the market and they moved away for a chat, heading in the direction of the bar.

"I bet you know most of the people here," said Jennifer. "Thanks to them being your customers."

"So do you, for the same reason! Of course I know Daniel and his family. Gwen and Erwan are getting everything ready outside," said Pippa. She looked out and could see Erwan talking to Meredith while carving the lamb with his father. Helpers were placing slices of lamb onto paper plates on a table next to them. It was like a finely tuned military operation.

"In fact, we should go over and congratulate Erwan, who's just been elected to the council," she added. "Although he's a bit distracted out there at the moment."

The two of them went out to join the queue which had formed behind Meredith to collect their dinner. They helped themselves to a rich mustard sauce which they poured over the meat, and each took two slices of bread to mop it up. There was room to sit down at the tables which Gwen had draped with paper tablecloths.

"Do you think this lamb had a name, before it was slaughtered?" said Pippa.

"You mean like Percy?" Jennifer laughed. "You're not getting squeamish, are you?"

They tucked into their meal, licking their lips which were covered in the sauce. "This is so delicious and tender," said Jennifer. She waved at Philippe, who was waiting to be served, and indicated that she'd kept him a chair beside her.

"Wait a sec," Pippa said. "You see that tall woman standing behind Philippe?"

"The hippy?"

"I wouldn't say that exactly," said Pippa, although she had to admit that many of the party guests were dressed alike in the casual Breton style of jeans and flowing tops.

"It's Louise. She's an art teacher. Shall I introduce you? She might take Mariam on."

"That's a great idea. Jonathan has already agreed to it. Is that her husband next to her?"

"Yes. Tegwenn. Although I've heard that he's a bit of a womaniser . . ."

As they continued to watch the couple, they saw Solenn pass by and stop to talk to Tegwenn. He stooped slightly to speak to her. His wife didn't join in the conversation and began to gaze around as though in search of other company.

"Oh. That's interesting," said Jennifer, watching the exchange.

"Do you think . . . ?" said Pippa. They both smiled.

After they finished eating, they took their drinks back into the barn where the violinist was encouraging the guests to dance. Pippa was swaying slightly and felt a little tipsy.

She noticed Louise get up from her table outdoors and said to Jennifer, "Come on, I'll introduce you to her."

Louise recognised Pippa, who said, "Louise, Jennifer. Jennifer, Louise." The two of them shook hands and Pippa explained about Jennifer's daughter.

"I would have time, yes, if you can bring her in the afternoon on the weekend," said Louise. "Once a week, is that what you're thinking?"

"Yes, if that works for you, it would be great," said Jennifer.

Louise replied that the classes would have to be on Sundays to fit in with her schedule. "I'm sorry, I can't manage during the week."

"That's fine," said Jennifer, hoping that it would be for both Mariam and Jonathan.

"How do you and Pippa know each other?" she asked Louise. "Are you a customer?"

"Not of Pippa, no. I live in Ploumenel and I go to Tristan and Madeleine's bakery."

"It's through an art connection," Pippa explained. "I explored joining a painting club for a while, which is how I met Louise, but in the end I didn't have time because of the bakery."

"Yes, it's a shame, it would have been fun. There are four of us who meet up regularly now," said Louise. One of the dancers came over and took her hand to pull her into a group which was now forming a circle.

"Excuse me," she said with a laugh.

Jennifer and Pippa moved back against the barn wall. "Do you want to join them?" Jennifer asked. Pippa shook her head.

"Maybe when Yann gets here," she replied, although she was starting to wonder when he might turn up.

"I had a chat with Bucky's wife earlier," she said, raising her voice over the noise of the partygoers. "My beef's not with her, after all. She seems nice."

"That's good. Any sign of your nemesis?" Jennifer asked.

"You mean Sylvie? I've not seen her. But I can't imagine her dancing in her state, can you?" They grinned.

Pippa continued to scan the guests. "That's one of Meredith's deputies, Christine, who's talking to Erwan. They know each other from the *mairie*, I suppose, but I'm surprised she's here. From what I gather there's no love lost between her and Daniel Le Floch's family."

Jennifer shrugged. "It's all part of the great tapestry of village life, isn't it? They come together and fall apart just like they're doing in this dance."

They fell silent to watch as the violinist played on, tapping his feet in time to the music. Solenn was dancing with an attractive woman, of about the same age, who was twirling with one hand in the air. At the end of the dance Solenn caught sight of Jennifer and Pippa and tapped her partner on the shoulder.

"Hello, ladies," she said. "This is my hairdresser, Annick."

"Congratulations," Jennifer said to Annick. "You do a great job," she added.

Annick smiled at the compliment. Pippa inspected her hairstyle more carefully. Her blonde highlights had been artfully curled with tongs.

"Where's your salon?" she asked.

"On the main street in Carhaix. You don't need a booking, if you're interested."

Pippa and Jennifer gave each other a meaningful look. Could this be *the* hairdresser presumed to have been one of Derek's lovers?

"Aren't you dancing?" Solenn asked. "Where's Yann?"

"He's on duty tonight," said Pippa, pulling a face.

A few minutes later, just after 10 p.m., Pippa's phone pinged. It was Yann, apologising. He wasn't going to make it. She wasn't surprised; Saturday nights in Carhaix were always busy for Yann when on duty, what with urban rodeos, drunks and drug dealers to contend with.

"Do you want another drink?" Jennifer asked.

Pippa hesitated. She knew why she'd started to drink too much. It was the stress.

"Actually, no thanks. Yann just let me know he's not coming, and it's late for me. I think I'd better go."

She touched her forehead. Her brow felt sweaty, and she was beginning to feel nauseous from the combination of the greasy meal and alcohol.

"Are you alright?" Jennifer asked. "Should you be driving?"

"I'm fine. Say goodbye to Philippe for me."

She drove home along the winding lanes in the dark at a snail's pace, terrified of falling into a ditch or bumping into a deer. She kept her headlights on full beam until she reached her cul de sac in Louennec, praying that she wouldn't get stopped by a gendarme on the lookout for Saturday night revellers. She smiled to herself at the thought that Yann was on duty that night.

She parked the car in the drive, opened the front door and dropped her bag in the hall. She ran straight up to her bathroom where she emptied the contents of her stomach, and immediately felt much better.

CHAPTER 29

"Come on," Jennifer said to Mariam after lunch the next day. "It's a lovely afternoon. We're going mushroom picking. It's peak season."

Mariam turned from her computer while she weighed up the invitation.

"What about Luke?" Mariam asked.

"He's staying here with Philippe." Jennifer batted away the first objection. Mariam could see that she wasn't going to be able to wriggle out of this.

"Can Pervenche come?"

"Not today, darling. We're going just the two of us. It's only a half hour drive and you can see her when we get back."

Jennifer had been thinking about her plan since the night before, and at least the weather was cooperating. But Mariam's brown eyes darkened as though she could sense a trap. It was unheard of for mother and daughter to go out together on a Sunday afternoon. Usually, it was Jonathan who would take the children on an outing to the coast when he was on weekend child duty. But the October weather was too unpredictable for that. Mariam turned back to her computer and switched it off, to the surprise of Jennifer who hadn't expected to win Round One so easily.

"Put your wellies on. With a bit of luck we'll find some ceps after the rain. Maybe Pervenche would like to come over for a yummy mushroom omelette later?" Jennifer went downstairs to pick up a basket, which would prevent the mushrooms from bruising, and took out a couple of small sharp knives from a kitchen drawer.

They got into the car, dressed in anoraks and boots, and set off along the track.

"Where are we going then?" Mariam wanted to know.

"To Huelgoat. I think Daddy took you once. But this time we're not hiking in the forest but combing the forest floor, just like in Merlin's time."

A faint smile lit up Mariam's oval face. She'd heard of the buried treasure left by Merlin the magician in the forest of Arthurian legend.

"Yes, but how do we know if the mushrooms are poisonous?" Mariam asked.

"First of all, we have to find some. We probably won't be the only ones mushroom hunting today, as they come up after rain. But as a general rule, I was always told the poisonous ones are the most attractive, like the red-capped ones. We're looking for the brown ones with brown gills. And if you're worried about one, don't pick it. OK?"

"OK." Mariam settled into silence again, but at least she wasn't sending out hostile vibes.

Jennifer filled the silence by nattering about the tasks in the market garden until they found a parking spot near a path leading into the forest.

"Here we are," she said brightly. They both took out a walking stick from the boot and began making their way through damp leaves under ancient oaks. After a while they left the path to explore the undergrowth.

"Use your stick to move the leaves away," Jennifer advised Mariam. "Sometimes they're hiding there, as they're the same colour as the leaves."

They advanced slowly, using the sticks like Geiger counters. From time to time, Mariam would ask, "Is this one?"

"No. Remember what I said. No white gills either. You'll soon get the hang."

They could hear the tinkle of a stream below them and the low afternoon sun illuminated their way. Moss-covered boulders were strewn down the slope as though hurled by a mythical giant.

"This is magical, isn't it?" said Jennifer. Mariam nodded, her head lowered as she searched for the hidden treasures. From time to time they would help each other over a slippery fallen log before examining underneath it.

"We'd better not get lost," Jennifer said. "Maybe we should go back to the path."

They climbed a little further, slithering through dead leaves, before turning back. Mariam stopped and looked around.

"It's so quiet, isn't it?" she said.

"Are you scared?"

"No. I meant in a nice way." As Mariam moved one foot, she dislodged some leaves and called out, "Mum, I think I've found some!"

Jennifer caught up with her, pushed the damp leaves away with her stick and saw four large mushrooms with fat stems.

"My God, these are ceps. Brilliant!"

She bent down with her knife and cut them at the base before dropping them into the basket. "These are in really good condition. Well done," she said. "And they're more than we'll need tonight."

"Are you sure they're edible ones?" Mariam asked.

"If you like we can find an open *pharmacie* in Huelgoat on the way home, to be on the safe side. Maybe have a cup of tea by the lake, too, if you like. But I'm pretty sure, yes."

Mariam kicked some more leaves away before asking, "What about these?"

Jennifer had seen those before. "You see the slightly yellow cap? They're death cap mushrooms. And they do what the name says."

They both laughed before retracing their steps back to the car, their eyes lowered to the undergrowth in case more of the boletes might be lurking there. But every time one of them stumbled on some fungi, Jennifer rejected them as unsafe.

"That was great," said Mariam, getting back into the car.

"Did you invite Pervenche over?" Jennifer asked.

"Not yet." Mariam called her friend and seemed to be having a long conversation in code until she rang off and said to Jennifer, "She's coming. Her mum will bring her after we get home."

They stopped off at a *pharmacie* in Huelgoat's pretty central square, and were reassured that they had indeed picked the mushroom king of the woods.

"Thank you, Mum," Mariam said on the way home. "I love that place."

Jennifer turned into Louennec from the main road and drove slowly past the *mairie*. A few cars were parked outside the church, whose bells were calling the faithful to mass.

She speeded up as they left the village perimeter and headed down a lane past Pascal's pig farm. By now she knew all the local farmers by name, and had seen several of them at the *méchoui*. She glanced across at Mariam before saying, "You know your drawings?"

Mariam was staring ahead and didn't reply. Jennifer decided to plough on.

"As I said to you, I think they're really good. Did you ever talk to Pippa?"

Mariam shook her head.

"I think you should show her. She's a proper artist and can help you."

Mariam still said nothing. She'd retreated into the habitual silence that Jennifer couldn't read. She gripped the steering wheel in frustration; she thought she'd made progress after their successful bonding session in the forest.

"What I mean is, she might give you some tips. Daddy and I are going to pay for you to have private lessons. In fact, I found you a teacher last night."

"Really?" Mariam turned her head to look at her.

"Yes, of course. Why not?" said Jennifer.

Mariam shook her shiny black hair in disbelief.

"That would be amazing. Thank you," she said.

"Well, put your best ones in your backpack tomorrow and I'll drop you off after school so you can talk it over with Pippa. She knows the painter who's offered to teach you."

They turned down the lane leading to the house. To Mariam's surprise, Jennifer pulled over and switched off the car.

"There's something else I wanted to mention, before we get home," she said. "You remember you were asking about your birth mother?"

"You mean in Daadab?" said Mariam.

What on earth was she talking about? Was she a mind reader?

"Yes, Daadab. How do you know that?"

Mariam raised her eyes to heaven. "It's all over social media," she said, in that patronising tone beloved of adolescents. "It was really easy to find the camp for Somali refugees. It's huge, actually."

"Yes, I know," said Jennifer. "I wrote to them."

She glanced sideways at Mariam who was grinning. "So did I!"

They turned to each other and exchanged a high five.

"But I wanted to tell you that I had a reply from the UN refugee agency. You see, I thought it was possible, although a long shot obviously, that your birth mother might have tried to track you down. Maybe years later. To find out what happened to you."

Mariam had turned to her and was listening intently. "And? I've not had a reply yet."

"Well, they don't have a record of her, but they're going to keep our details on file. It's not much, but it might not be hopeless, I suppose. Is that OK?"

Mariam was staring down the lane where golden leaves were fluttering to the ground. What was she thinking?

"I want to donate," she said. "I want to get involved. They have a donate button on their site and I'm going to wash cars or something like that to add to my pocket money. I might even do a collection at school."

Jennifer reached over to give her daughter a kiss on the cheek. What an elegant solution she'd found to connect with her people in a foreign land. And such a positive way to deal with her existential uncertainty. She was sure that Jonathan would approve.

"Wow," she said. "That's a brilliant idea. And do you know what? However much you raise, Daddy and I will double the amount. How does that sound?"

"It sounds great. Thank you."

CHAPTER 30

Pippa had just opened the boot to take out her shopping when the sound of a car horn made her jump.

"Need a hand?" Jennifer had wound down her car window and Mariam was stepping out from the passenger side.

"Mariam can help me," Pippa said. "Come on."

"I'll pick her up in an hour, if that's OK?" said Jennifer, before turning the car round at the end of the cul de sac.

Mariam and Pippa carted the bags of shopping inside and installed themselves at the kitchen table.

"I don't think you've ever been inside my house, in all this time?" Pippa said. She offered to make some tea, which Mariam accepted shyly.

"Let's have a look at your stuff," Pippa said.

Mariam leaned down from her chair and took out a sheaf of paper from her backpack, which she placed on the table. Pippa brought over two mugs of tea with some milk.

"Did you have a nice weekend?"

"Mum and I went to Huelgoat," said Mariam.

"Ah. Did you see the huge round stones in the woods? The Gargantua stone?"

"No, not that one. But we weren't hiking."

"So you didn't see the trembling rock?"

"What trembling rock?" Mariam asked.

"*Le rocher tremblant*. It's a long granite boulder which is perfectly balanced, but it means that with very little effort even a child can push it up slightly. You should check out the videos on TikTok."

Mariam grinned. "OK, I will. But we went mushroom picking, probably in another part of the forest. It was super cool."

"What did you find? Any ceps?"

"Oh yes. It's the peak season. But it's hard to tell which are the ones you can eat, and which are the poisonous ones."

"Yes. Best to check with someone who knows."

"That's what we did."

"May I?" Pippa gestured to the pile of paper and picked up the top sheet. It was an intricate drawing of a lime tree leaf, its veins clearly shown. The sheet below, in colour, showed an anemone drawn with the minute detail of a botanist.

"Are these recent?" she asked. Mariam nodded.

"Are you sure you've never had any lessons?" Pippa asked. "These are extremely good."

"Thank you. Mum said you'd show me some of yours."

"Well. Where do you want to start? I don't have that much time for painting and drawing here, but I could show you some from when I was in London. I used to go to the forest for inspiration, but I always try to put a narrative into mine. You'll see what I mean."

She got up and went into the living room, returning with her own pile.

"This one, for example. It's a watercolour." Mariam scrutinised the painting, which showed a little boy with huge eyes looking at the viewer from behind a tree.

"Is he happy? I can't tell."

"I think so. If you look in the corner here, there's another boy. They were playing hide and seek when I painted them."

"I see. So you're telling a story."

Pippa nodded.

"I did that too," said Mariam. She shuffled through her pile and pulled out a drawing from near the bottom. Two girls were in a playground, behind railings. One was veiled, and the other was holding her arm.

"Is that you?" Pippa asked, pointing to the veiled figure.

Mariam gave a faint nod of the head while still staring at the two figures.

"And is that girl hurting you? Is she squeezing your arm?"

"They called me Mariam musulmane. And I found out that some Muslim girls dress like that."

"Yes, I know. But not you. They were afraid of you because you were different," said Pippa. "And cleverer."

Mariam smiled. "Thank you."

Pippa put her arm round Mariam's shoulder, and the girl leaned in.

"Anyway, that's all in the past now," said Pippa. "But you're creative. You wanted to put your feelings down on paper to express yourself in that way. I think that it's great you'll be taking private lessons, and Louise Le Roux is a very good teacher. I'm sure you'll like her."

* * *

Pippa's first customer the next morning was Gwen's brother, Erwan. He was small and stocky, in contrast to his taller younger sister.

"Congratulations on your election!" Pippa said across the counter. "Did you enjoy the party? You were surrounded by so many people that I couldn't get to you."

"Thank you." He grinned.

"Meredith will be counting on you."

He grinned. "I know. Let's say there are different views on the council, which is pretty much divided into two camps."

"You're dead right there," said Pippa. "Meredith's and Sylvie's."

"For some reason, I have the impression that Sylvie didn't back me," he said with a grimace.

"Who cares? You won! What can I get you?" she asked.

He opted for a *pain au chocolat* and wished her a cheerful "*Bonne journée*" as he headed off to the village school.

No sooner had he left than the door opened again. A buxom middle-aged woman wearing a mac and a colourful scarf on her head came in for a baguette. Pippa immediately recognised Madame Briand's Portuguese carer. Her jowls were heavy and her skin weather beaten.

"*Bonjour, Madame. Mes condoléances*," Pippa said, as though the woman had lost a relative. Maybe the death of her employer had been a bit like that, she thought. She wondered if the two had been close.

"*Merci.*"

Pippa couldn't help asking about the death scene. "I heard that Madame Briand choked to death . . . ?" She refrained from mentioning the baguette issue.

"Yes. She was having soup and somehow a piece of baguette became caught in her windpipe. It was all over in seconds," the woman said, displaying no emotion, and speaking with a strong accent.

"I'm so sorry to hear that. *Une tradition?*" she asked.

"You mean was the choking a tradition? I'm sorry, I don't understand."

"No, I mean would you like a baguette *tradition?*" Pippa asked.

"Oh yes. *Pas trop cuite s'il vous plait.*"

Pippa took out a suitably undercooked loaf and waited while the carer swiped her debit card.

"Had she been in poor health generally?"

The woman seemed to bristle. She replied, "Oh no, she was in very good health."

She turned to go, but Pippa wanted to know about the funeral details.

"It's this afternoon. There won't be many people," the woman said. "Monsieur le curé has organised it. He was a good friend of Madame."

"She no longer has any family, I understand."

"And she was old. Nobody came to visit her while I worked there."

"And how long was that?" Pippa was afraid that her questioning was too intrusive, but the woman replied, "Six months."

"And do you live in Louennec?"

She hesitated before replying that she lived on the village outskirts, with an arm gesture which left the location vague. Pippa was starting to feel awkward about pressing her any further.

"Well, enjoy the baguette. Maybe see you later," she said, with a bright smile.

Pippa thought back over the conversation as Gwen breezed in and went straight into the back. Something didn't add up, but she didn't know what. Madame Briand's carer had just confirmed that she'd choked to death on a piece of baguette. Yet hadn't Madame Briand told her that on the night before her death she'd had a tummy upset?

Pippa then recalled Mariam mentioning that it was peak mushroom time. It might be nothing, but what if . . . ?

She took out her phone and began googling *poisonous mushrooms*.

CHAPTER 31

Pippa was serving a customer when they heard the church bells toll from across the street to summon the mourners to Madame Briand's funeral.

"The poor lady," said the customer, popping her baguette into a bag. "But she had a good life."

Pippa nodded sagely as though in agreement, although she knew perfectly well that this was only half true.

"Are you going to the funeral?" she asked. She gestured towards the street, which was dampened by rain. Only a small group of people had trickled inside. Maybe it was because of the weather, Pippa thought. But then most of Madame Briand's friends had probably died.

"I didn't really know her," the customer admitted. "Even though she'd lived in Louennec for many years."

Pippa asked Gwen if she'd mind holding the fort while she slipped across to the church. She'd been a loyal customer after all, and she wanted to pay her respects.

She sat at the back next to a young woman who seemed to know her and who greeted her warmly. Pippa smiled and shook her hand, racking her brains until she remembered she was the local notary who had helped her with the administrative hurdles when taking over the bakery lease.

The priest, the same elderly curé who had officiated at Derek's funeral, was intoning a homage to the dead woman in his monotonous stage whisper. But unlike at Derek's funeral, he made it clear that he and Madame Briand had been friends.

He stressed how her faith had carried her through life. "She lived according to the teaching of Christ by putting the interests of others before herself," he said, surveying the sparse congregation as though exhorting them to do the same.

"I think many people may not be aware of this, but when Madame Briand arrived in Louennec before marrying her husband here, she was the *directrice* of the village school," he went on. "Not only did she keep in touch with many of her pupils, but after her retirement she coached individuals who went on to be extremely successful in the life of our country." He cited one who became a government minister and another the mayor of Rennes.

"Simone Briand was proud to have received the Légion d'honneur in her later years for raising the educational level of the Bretons, and for her devotion to public service," he said.

"Of course, following the untimely death of her husband, Simone withdrew from public life," he added. "But she attended church until she passed away."

Why hadn't the priest taken matters into his own hands to help her, Pippa wondered. He must surely have been aware of what was going on at the house. But then why would he? She had no faith in the Catholic Church's ability to save any souls.

Only a few mourners took up the priest's invitation to take communion, apart from the inevitable group of elderly villagers dressed in black who appeared from nowhere as they did at every funeral. He then gave the final blessing and the coffin was carried past the pews out to the cemetery as the organist played a dirge.

Pippa stood under the porch for a moment chatting with the notary, while they waited for the rain to ease.

"*Ce n'est qu'un grain,*" said the notary to reassure her, referring to the passing downpours that were the hallmark of that time of year. Pippa had noticed that Bretons discussed the weather as much as Brits.

"Did you know Madame Briand had the Légion?" Pippa asked her.

The woman shook her head. "I didn't know any of that. She was obviously a good person. It was a tragedy, the wrangling over the inheritance," she commented.

"Ah yes, I suppose you would know all about that from your job?" said Pippa.

"Of course." The notary hesitated, as though wondering whether to pursue the conversation. "Everyone knew what was going on, but nobody wanted to interfere," she added with a sigh. Pippa remembered how she'd tried to intervene herself after once hearing an altercation from across the street, but to no avail.

"I was sorry to see that you received a poison pen letter regarding Madame Briand's death," the notary said.

"Thank you. Yes, it was very upsetting."

"I'm not sure whether I should mention this to you, but I must tell you something in confidence."

Pippa could sense the hairs on her neck prickling with tension.

"Just before her death, Madame Briand changed her will. I was surprised when she came to my office, and even more surprised by her decision."

Pippa leaned closer. "Why, what did she decide? Did she leave everything to charity? Or to the Church? When did she do this?"

The notary smiled.

"No. She didn't do anything like that. I was surprised that she left her entire estate to her carer. And so, when she died only a few days later, I did wonder . . ."

CHAPTER 32

Pippa crossed the street and returned to the bakery, her brain churning.

Had Madame Briand been pressured by the carer to change her will? That seemed to be the obvious conclusion. But then Pippa had a darker thought in the light of her conversation with the notary. Once the carer had persuaded her employer to leave the estate to her, all she had to do was ensure her early demise . . . which had happened only a matter of days later.

Pippa's heart began to pound with excitement. That afternoon she hardly paid attention to what her customers were ordering. She ended up in a tense exchange with one who started arguing about what he'd received in his lucky dip from the app.

"Monsieur, I believe we've told you before that you get our leftovers at the end of the day at knockdown prices only because you can't choose yourself what we put in the bag," she said loudly, so that everyone could hear. The young man, embarrassed, paid up and slunk out. She almost called after him to apologise, but she'd wanted to teach him a lesson. She'd already complained to Gwen about youngsters trying to break the rules, and by this time villagers were queueing for their daily baguette after work.

Pippa couldn't wait to shut the shop that evening so that she could get home to tell Yann what she'd learned.

But how could she betray the notary's confidence?

* * *

Pippa pulled down the bakery shutters at seven thirty sharp and wandered along to her cul de sac.

As she walked down her street, she began scrutinising the front doors of the residents. What if the police had missed someone who might have seen the anonymous letter-writer posting it through her letterbox? They must have more pressing investigations on their plate, she thought.

She almost gasped when she noticed a video doorbell on the house right opposite her own. A young couple who worked in Carhaix lived there with their two children. They'd put up a basketball hoop above the garage door for the elder child, and the toys of the younger one were often strewn in the front garden.

Pippa rang the doorbell and a harried-looking woman opened the door. Pippa immediately recognised her as one of her customers.

"I'm so sorry to disturb you." She pointed to her own house. "I live opposite. I should have introduced myself ages ago, particularly as your daughter likes my apple turnovers. I'm Pippa."

"Yes. Same here, we're all so busy, aren't we? I'm Morgane. Sorry, we're just giving the kids something to eat. How can I help? We had the gendarmes here the other day asking us about your poison pen letter."

Why had Yann never mentioned this to her? Pippa felt foolish standing in front of the door.

"Were you able to help?" she asked, pointing at the digital doorbell.

"*Pff*," Morgane replied. "*C'est un cauchemar, ses trucs-là.*"

Why were they a nightmare? Pippa had never thought of buying one because of the risk of being hacked, but otherwise she couldn't see a downside.

"Why?" she asked.

"The slightest thing would set it off. Particularly in the evening, when we're at home, of course. A gust of wind, or a car doing a three-point turn. And the kids playing outside in the front, that was the last straw. It drove me mad. So my husband disabled it a couple of weeks ago."

Pippa couldn't conceal her disappointment. She remembered the car which had unnerved her doing a three-point turn in her own drive in the darkness, but there was no point in mentioning that now.

"A couple of weeks ago? Are you sure? Maybe it was more recently?"

"I'm sorry, Peeper. It was at least two weeks ago. I hope they find *le corbeau*," Morgane said. "You must come over to meet the family one day soon, when it's quieter," she added, before shutting the door gently.

Pippa crossed the street to her house, wondering whether Yann might have caught sight of her from the other side. Her eyes slid over to his house where his car was parked. Was that his shadow moving behind the living room blind? A moment later, his front door opened.

She smiled and approached his house.

"Peeper," he said, in a reproachful voice, "I told you about not interfering in police work."

"Yes, I know. I'm sorry."

"Are you coming in?" He held open the door and she stepped inside. They kissed each other on the cheeks.

"Just for a moment. I wanted to tell you what I heard today."

He laughed, leaning against the wall in the hall. "What else have you been up to?"

She stiffened at the implied criticism. "I just happened to talk to the local notary about Madame Briand at her funeral. She thinks it may not be a coincidence that the old lady changed her will just before she died."

"Did she?" He stroked his chin. "Very interesting."

"Erm, except that she told me that in confidence."

Yann frowned. "I see. Notaries are bound by solicitor-client privilege. It sounds like she suspected Madame Briand of being forced to change her will, but that is all."

"Can't you get a magistrate to intervene?" Pippa insisted.

"In this case? Maybe, maybe not," said Yann. But he looked dubious.

"I heard that she employed the carer after having a fall a few months ago. And so now I've started to think: what if she fell *after* the carer arrived?"

"You mean what if the carer pushed her? And then abused this vulnerable woman?" said Yann. "Isn't there a history of abuse in that family?"

"Yes, exactly," Pippa replied. "Not only that, but what if she poisoned her too, after forcing her to change her will."

"Poisoned? What are you talking about?" He sighed.

"Did I mention that I saw her on the morning of her death? She told me that the night before she'd had stomach pains. This is a woman who was in perfectly good health, according to what her carer told me. Then the next day she dies . . . don't you think that there could be a connection, and that the symptoms from eating poisonous mushrooms might be examined? Particularly as she died only a few days after changing the will!"

"But Peeper," Yann replied, "she was an old lady. This is all very well, but can you expect us to dig up her body for tests after she has just been buried? There's a strong chance that any traces of poisoning would have disappeared by now. Will you come in?" he asked, gesturing towards the kitchen. She sensed his mounting irritation and said she had to go home.

Then he added, "What we need is proof." He waved one hand in the air. "Not just suspicions."

CHAPTER 33

The stone cottage in Ploumenel was set back from the road. Mariam looked across at Jennifer nervously as she parked by the wall.

Tegwenn, wearing a Breton stripe, was cutting the grass in the front garden. Observing his slim build, chiselled jawline and neatly trimmed beard, it was easy for Jennifer to understand the physical attraction that might have drawn Solenn to him.

"Don't worry, you'll be fine," Jennifer said to Mariam. She called out "*Bonjour*" to Tegwenn, who waved without stopping his lawnmower. They walked to the front door, which was opened by Louise who welcomed them inside.

"Wasn't that fun, last weekend?" she said to Jennifer. She was dressed in the same style of loose top and distressed jeans that she had worn at the *méchoui*. "So you must be Mariam. I've heard a lot about you from your *maman*."

Jennifer sensed that Mariam must be squirming inside with embarrassment at the attention. She'd wanted to deliver her to the first class to make sure all went well. Jonathan had readily agreed as it gave him time for a Sunday round of golf.

"We've brought some of Mariam's drawings to show you," Jennifer began. They were standing in a low-ceilinged living room where artwork was displayed on the walls. The furniture was comfortable, with throws strewn on two armchairs and a modest sofa of a different design. Jennifer was reminded of her own furniture at home, which had been picked up from local flea markets. There were a few photos on the mantelpiece, but no sign of any children.

"Are these all by you?" Jennifer asked. She pointed to a couple of oil paintings on the wall.

"Not all, but some, yes," said Louise. "Those two are."

Jennifer admired the painting on the wall above the fireplace. It was a bleak and wind-whipped landscape, a finger of land being attacked by ocean breakers seething with white spume.

"Is that the Pointe du Raz?" she asked.

"Yes. The wind was so strong that day that it was impossible to work with my easel. I ended up taking photos and painted it here. Have you been?"

"Yes. We went on a lovely afternoon, didn't we?" she said, turning to Mariam, who nodded. "We stood looking out to sea and thinking, the next land across the ocean is America."

Louise had noticed a ginger cat stretched out on an armchair and clapped her hands to get him down: "*Descends*, Genghis!" she instructed, gesturing to the floor, but the cat ignored her.

"That's the trouble with these barn cats, they just do what they like," she complained. She went to the front window and looked out. "Weren't we lucky with the weather at the party? At least it's not raining so far today. I've put Tegwenn to work before it starts again. Shall we go through?"

She led the way via a small kitchen to the back door, which opened onto a courtyard. A converted barn with large windows cut into the sloping roof stood at the far side.

"This is my studio." Louise pushed open the door and they stepped inside. The entire barn was suffused with natural light. Mariam began to explore the space where paintings of all different sizes — portraits and landscapes — were hanging or propped against the walls. A couple of easels stood next to tables where oil paints and cloths lay. A large half-finished portrait of a woman kneading dough was displayed on one. The woman looked familiar. A table displaying ceramics, studded with Breton symbols, stood in a corner.

"You're a potter as well as a painter?" Jennifer asked.

"Oh yes. The kiln is outside," Louise explained. "It's in a shed in the courtyard."

"I have a friend who makes Breton jewellery. I think you know her, actually. Solenn. She has a market stall in Carhaix," said Jennifer, remembering too late the interaction between Solenn and Tegwenn at the *méchoui*.

"Solenn? Oh yes, I know her," said Louise. Her mouth gave the slightest twitch.

Jennifer added, quickly, "So, I'm going to leave Mariam with you. Shall I pick her up in two hours, as we agreed?"

Jennifer called out to Mariam, "Is that alright?"

Mariam turned round from a picture she was examining, and smiled. "Sure," she said.

Jennifer sneaked another look at the portrait in progress. The blonde woman making bread was in a white apron and her hair was tied back. "Isn't that Madeleine from the bakery?" she asked.

"Yes it's her. I'm still working on it. I've been working from photographs, but I've also sat watching her and Tristan shaping the dough in the back."

Mariam was still looking round the studio, entranced. Louise cleared space on a table, before saying to her, "Right, Mariam, let's look at your work and see what we can do today."

CHAPTER 34

The next week passed uneventfully, for which Jennifer was grateful.

There were no moods or tantrums from either child, who both helped out in the garden without being asked. She gave Mariam ten euros for washing the mud off her car, and then thought she'd been overly generous. She found time between assignments for the paper to do the hoovering and shake out the dog hairs from kitchen rugs. In the evenings, once the children had gone to bed, she and Philippe even found the time to chill on the sofa in front of the TV.

When market day came round, Jennifer was proud of her produce on sale. She handed a celeriac to Meredith and waited while she examined the vegetable in all its ugliness.

"It's so big. And heavy," Meredith said, raising her hand in an exaggerated way as though the vegetable was too heavy to carry.

Jennifer smiled. Something made her look across at the bakery stall owned by Pippa's rival. Unusually, that morning, there was no sign of Bucky or Madeleine, and the space for their stall was empty.

"It's incredibly versatile, though. I like it grated in salads. Or diced in soup. It gives it a taste of celery and parsley, very subtle," she said.

"Really?" said Meredith. "I only thought of making *céleri rémoulade*."

"Of course, yes, why not? With homemade mayonnaise," said Jennifer. "Take one and try the different things you can do. I should have even more pumpkins next week too, also good in soup."

"Good, it's almost Halloween," said Meredith. She held out a ten euro note, which also paid for her eggs, some apples and a bunch of dahlias. "Thank you, my dear," she said, before putting her purchases in her shopping bag and moving along to Pippa for some bread. Pippa had a queue waiting, and was handing some croissants to a young man in a leather jacket who looked as though he'd just got out of bed.

The other farm stalls were piled high with colourful fruit and vegetables. Some displayed yellow girolles mushrooms.

Jennifer's favourite time of year was marred only by the weather. The October storms hit Finistère with their full force after barrelling across the Atlantic, just like in the picture in Louise's living room.

Solenn was back, looking as glamorous as ever behind her little jewellery stall, and was chatting with a grey-haired guy who looked vaguely familiar. Something in the way they were talking, leaning towards each other, made Jennifer wonder whether they were more intimate than friends. The man reached out to touch Solenn on the shoulder before kissing her goodbye. As he turned to go, Jennifer remembered having been introduced after Derek's funeral. Was it Gabriel? Could he be one of Solenn's lovers? Jennifer remembered what Pippa had said about Solenn's conduct after Derek died. Would she have been capable of committing a murder to be with a lover? Or what if the murderer was Gabriel in a fit of jealous pique? Jennifer shook off the whole idea as being too far-fetched.

But the tangled relations in their small village were endless, she thought, including in her own marriage. Unlike Solenn, though, she'd never been able to separate sex from love.

Pippa called to Jennifer from her stall, awakening her from her reverie.

"You ready?" She pointed in the direction of the Central Café.

"Give me five," said Jennifer, holding up her hand. It was one o'clock and Philippe was already strolling to the café with Jean-Luc for their regular lunchtime drink. But she wanted to buy some girolles on her way there. Mariam might be persuaded to eat some after the excitement of their mushroom hunt. Although when cooked with garlic and parsley, if you closed your eyes, you could almost mistake the fleshy girolles for meat.

The café was busy and they squeezed through the lunchtime throng just as a couple were leaving a table where the waiter agreed to serve them a quick cup of coffee.

Pippa rubbed her hands. "It's nippy out, isn't it?"

"Yes, it sure is. Look at these . . ." She showed Pippa her paper bag containing the girolles.

"Mmm, what a treat," Pippa said, sniffing them. "The price has started to come down because they're so plentiful."

"What's happening?" Jennifer asked.

"Nothing since I told you about the big question mark over what happened to Madame Briand, and my theory about mushroom poisoning. Still nothing on the poison pen writer, either, if that's what you mean," Pippa replied. "Except that in my mind, it's still Sylvie. She's had it in for me since I arrived."

"It might take time, but I'm sure the cops will get the person who did that. I mean, it's such a small village, Louennec," said Jennifer. "I've had a pretty quiet week too," she added. She cupped her hand round her coffee for warmth. "Mariam washed my car, and did Jonathan's too, as well as going round to a couple of neighbouring farmers, in her drive to help Somali refugees."

Jennifer had already briefed Pippa on the initiative and she nodded her appreciation. "You can send her round to me, you know. I bet she could make a fortune on my street."

Jennifer glanced round to make sure they weren't being overheard. She leaned closer to Pippa and said in a quiet voice, "I didn't tell Mariam the whole story about my reply from the refugee camp, by the way."

Pippa raised an eyebrow.

"Do you remember I told you that she was found outside the camp by the roadside? Well, when they saw that Mariam was a few months old when that happened, they said that was unusual. I found out separately that it seems that if babies are left outside the camp it's likely to be a teenage mother who leaves a newborn out of shame."

"Out of shame? Oh no . . . I can only imagine."

Jennifer gripped Pippa's arm. "Yes. How awful. The good news though is that they seem to think that Mariam must have arrived with a family group who came across during the unrest in Somalia. Maybe the mother couldn't cope with a large family and a baby. But I guess we'll never know."

She sighed and reached for her coffee. Pippa gave her a sympathetic glance before changing the subject.

"What about the art class? How did it go?"

"Oh yes. Thanks again for putting us in touch with Louise. It went really well. Mariam had the first lesson last Sunday."

"Good. How often is she going?"

"Once a week. I'm taking her there again tomorrow."

"They have a nice place, using the old barn as a studio. Was Tegwenn there?" Pippa asked with a smile.

"Yes he was. He was cutting the grass when we arrived, but we didn't talk."

"You'll see that he oozes charm," said Pippa. "When he talks, it's like he's pouring dark chocolate all over you."

Jennifer laughed. "It sounds as though you have a thing for him. I can see the attraction. He's not bad looking."

"Not me, no. But that wouldn't stop someone like Solenn, would it?"

"Exactly!" said Jennifer.

As she spoke, she sensed somebody standing behind her. She turned round and looked up to see Philippe.

"Jennifer," he said, urgently.

"What's the matter?" she asked.

"Tristan is dead," he said. For a moment Jennifer couldn't remember a Tristan.

"Who?" she asked him again.

It was Pippa who replied. "Bucky. He means Bucky. What happened?"

"He's just been found dead in his bakery!"

CHAPTER 35

Pippa slumped back in her chair. "Oh no!" she exclaimed.

"I heard it was a customer who discovered the body this morning," said Philippe.

Pippa shook her head in disbelief. "God, I didn't like him, but I didn't want him to die. Poor Madeleine."

"That would explain why there was nobody at their stall this morning. She must be distraught," said Jennifer. She asked Philippe, "Who told you?"

"One of my friends in his village. But everyone knows now," he said. Jennifer became aware of phones pinging around them. She looked round the café and it seemed as though all the customers were on the phone with sorrowful expressions on their faces.

"News certainly travels fast round here. Thanks for telling us," she said to Philippe, with a rueful smile, and he returned to his group of friends at the bar.

"Wouldn't you expect Yann to have let you know?" she asked Pippa.

"He'd never do that. Even if it involved someone I know. I'm sure I'll find out from him, but not until we next see each other."

"I wonder what happened," said Jennifer. "Might he have killed himself?"

"Who knows? I guess we'll find out soon enough." Pippa began gathering her things together. "First Derek. Now Bucky. And Madame Briand too. What on earth is going on round here?" she said, before adding, "Do you mind paying? I've got to get back to the bakery."

* * *

Pippa noticed a huddle of customers in front of the counter when she pushed open the door. As soon as Gwen saw her, they all fell silent and Gwen began handing out bread and cakes as the women formed an orderly queue to pay.

"Did you hear?" Gwen asked Pippa.

"About Tristan? Yes I did. It's very sad news, and terrible for Madeleine," she replied. The customers, interrupted in full flow, were now paying their bills before filing out.

Pippa noticed they resumed their conversation as soon as they got out onto the pavement. She imagined that all sorts of wild theories must be doing the rounds.

"Do you know what happened?" Pippa asked Gwen. "I heard that one of Tristan's customers found him in the bakery."

Gwen seemed to be taking the news hard, leaning against the counter for support. Pippa noticed a tear on her cheek and gave her a hug.

"Was he a friend of yours?" she asked.

"No, Madame. My family knew him and Madeleine, of course," she said. "Do you think somebody is targeting bakers?"

"Why? Are you scared? I'm sure there's no need for that." Pippa tried to reassure the young woman and put an arm round her. But she was worried about the same thing herself.

"Why would anyone do this? Maybe he killed himself," she said.

"But I was told that when the gendarmes came, he had a head wound and breadcrumbs were scattered near his body." Gwen stared at Pippa with her eyes wide.

Pippa didn't need to be reminded that Derek had suffered the same fate. She didn't voice her thoughts to Gwen, but what had happened to Bucky was chilling. *Who was committing these baguette murders?* she wondered.

CHAPTER 36

Before shutting up shop that evening, Pippa took a moment to pass on her condolences to Madeleine.

Madeleine answered the phone immediately but spoke in a small voice, as though she was ill.

"I'm just calling to say how sorry I am about Tristan," Pippa began. "I can only imagine how you must feel."

"Thank you, Peeper. Yes. It was my friend Louise who found him. I didn't go to the market because I didn't have the strength," she replied.

"If there's anything I can do just let me know," said Pippa before ringing off. It seemed there was nothing else to say, apart from her disbelief that a killer would target a baker, even a horrible one like Bucky. *What if she was next?*

She pulled down the shutters and began making her way home. She felt as though everything was piling up around her, and the feeling wasn't good.

In fact, she thought, she hadn't felt so low since she'd taken out a discrimination suit against her French bank in London after a more junior Frenchman was promoted above her. She'd ended up winning the case, but the downside of the verdict was the harm to her reputation, which had meant that she could never work in investment banking again. She was trouble, she'd heard it whispered.

Now the whispers against her had started again and she was powerless to stop them. She looked at her watch. The evening stretching ahead of her was a blank slate. Yann was working that night and they'd arranged to see each other in two days' time, on her day off.

As she passed the church, she noticed that the door was ajar. She'd only entered the building for funerals, but maybe she could just sit quietly by herself to calm the intrusive thoughts that had troubled her all day, since learning of Bucky's death.

The church was dimly lit and she walked to the front pew where she sat down to think things through.

After a few minutes she heard footsteps, and turned round. The elderly curé, who'd conducted the funerals of Derek and Madame Briand, was coming towards her. She turned away to face the front and the small stained-glass window behind the altar.

"*Bonsoir, Madame,*" he said. "You are seeking solitude? Peace of mind, perhaps?"

"Oh. Well, I suppose I am," she said. "I've not had a good day."

He stretched out a hand. "I believe you are the lady who runs the bakery opposite?"

She nodded, shaking his hand. "That's right. Pippa Sinclair." She pronounced her last name the French way, *Sanclair*, as usual. "I was at Madame Briand's funeral the other day. She was one of my customers."

"Very sad, yes. She was a pillar of the community. A big loss, and for me personally. May I?"

He gestured towards the pew. She hadn't expected, or even wanted, company, but she shuffled over so that he could sit next to her. They both contemplated the stained-glass window showing an angel hovering above Jesus, whose head was bowed under the crown of thorns, gesturing towards heaven.

She cast a sideways glance at the priest. It was the first time she'd seen him without his robes, and he was dressed in dark trousers and a turtleneck sweater under a jacket. In profile, he had a hook nose and his sparse hair was arranged in a comb-over.

"What is troubling you, Madame, if I may ask?" He turned to face her.

Was this a confessional? Pippa felt uneasy.

"I don't want to burden you, *mon père*," she said. "But did you hear about the death of Tristan Trobellec?"

He nodded. "The baker? I did indeed. Very distressing. You knew him well? I suppose you did, in your line of business."

"We weren't actually friends, no. Rivals, more like." She didn't intend to say more, but couldn't help adding, "In fact he accused me of sabotaging his bakery, completely falsely, I should tell you."

The curé said nothing and Pippa felt emboldened to continue. She hoped there was nobody else in the church as she raised her voice.

"I think my problem is that I'm upset by what's happening in the village. As you know, my friend Derek Cooper was killed a few weeks ago—"the curé nodded acknowledgement — "but now there are rumours about me being a police informer, and I've been accused of killing Madame Briand with my baguettes! I feel terrible. I should say that all these accusations are completely false and slanderous!"

"Killing her?" He sat up straight and looked her in the eyes.

Pippa poured out the story of her visit to Sylvie Le Goff while the priest listened, rapt. Then, after a moment's hesitation, she also mentioned her conversation with the notary after the old lady's funeral.

He remained still, contemplating the window before them, then said, "You say that *Madame la notaire* suspected the carer of hastening Madame Briand's death so that she could inherit her estate?"

"Yes, that's exactly what I'm saying."

A long silence ensued. Pippa sensed that he knew something.

"*Mon père?*" she asked.

"This is a matter to do with the *secret confessionnel*," he said, with a shrug.

"You mean that Madame Briand confessed something to you, and you don't have the right to pass it on?"

He sighed. "That is exactly right, Madame."

She wasn't going to let him get away with that. "*Mon père*, I understand that these days if a crime has been committed, the law must prevail. Have you never mentioned this to the gendarmerie?"

"Madame, this is the first I've heard about the suspicions of the notary. I would say that it does correspond to what Madame Briand told me at confession before her death, however."

Pippa's heart was beating fit to burst. "Well, in that case, I really think that you should mention this to the police so that justice can be done!" she exclaimed.

Again, he said nothing. But she noticed his eyes were fixed on the cross standing on the altar, as though seeking counsel from God.

Pippa had said enough. She picked up her handbag and wished him a *bonne soirée*.

She turned into her cul de sac and walked slowly along to her house in the dusk. As she turned the key in the front door, she heard a car approach. It had *gendarmerie* marked in a white stripe along the side and she presumed it would stop outside Yann's house.

But the car came to a halt at the end of her drive. She recognised the female gendarme in the passenger seat who had been called to the scene of Derek's death.

"Madame Pippa Sinclair?" the woman asked, rolling down the window.

"Yes."

"Please come with us. We would like you to come to the gendarmerie to help us with our inquiries," she said.

CHAPTER 37

Pippa hesitated for a moment. What could this be about?

She knew she couldn't refuse, and as she stepped into the car she could swear she saw a curtain twitch in the house opposite, where Morgane and her family lived. She was mortified to think that news of her being picked up by a police car would soon be all around the village.

She leaned forward and said to the woman, "You are Madame Gallou, yes? I remember you."

"*Maréchal des logis-chef* Maguy Gallou, yes, Madame," she replied. Was it only an impression, or was her tone more formal than when they'd first met, Pippa wondered.

"Can you please tell me what this is about? I'm sure there must be a misunderstanding," she stammered.

"As you know, Madame, Monsieur Tristan Trobellec was killed at his bakery in Ploumenel this morning, and we believe that you may be able to help us with our inquiries."

Pippa was at a loss as to why they wanted to talk to her. Maguy had turned back to face the road and clearly didn't want to engage in conversation until they reached the gendarmerie in Carhaix. Pippa wondered whether Yann was part of the investigation and was terrified of bumping into him as they walked up the steps to the entrance.

She was led into a small interview room where Maguy and a male gendarme, introduced as an adjudant, sat opposite her at a table. After checking her identification and informing her that they were being recorded, Maguy began by asking where she had been that morning.

"I was at the market. Like every Saturday," she replied, as calmly as possible.

"At what time?" the man asked.

"I must have left home about eight thirty," she said. "Yes, that's right, because I need to get my stall ready for nine."

"Eight thirty? Are you sure?" the man asked, leaning forward.

"Yes. Why?"

"Can anybody confirm that?"

"Well, I'm not sure. I live by myself, you see . . ." she began. She was starting to feel flustered. Were they trying to trap her?

"You are the owner of a red Renault Mégane, are you not?" the adjudant asked. Judging by his cocky attitude, he appeared to be Maguy's superior.

Where was this going? Pippa wondered. "Yes, I am. Why?"

"Because that car was seen outside Monsieur Trobellec's bakery this morning at about eight thirty."

"How do you know it was my car? It definitely wasn't me, if that's what you mean," said Pippa, raising her voice. "Who says they saw it? Did they see the number plate?"

The two gendarmes pulled a face and looked at each other before Maguy replied.

"We cannot tell you who reported this, Madame. So you deny having been in the vicinity at that time this morning."

"Yes of course I do! It's not on my way to Carhaix and I had no reason to stop off there."

The two gendarmes tried another tack.

"You will recall that we met after the sad death of one of your friends," Maguy said.

"Derek Cooper. Yes," Pippa replied. Her heart sank. The police were obviously making a connection between the two murders.

"Well, as you will remember, the weapon that killed your friend was a metal rod inside a baguette. And you are a baker and were the first person to arrive on the scene of your friend's death. You also telephoned him on the morning of his death. In addition, we are aware that you had a serious dispute with Monsieur Trobellec. I can tell you that we found breadcrumbs around the body and we are searching for the murder weapon. Our scientists believe that the head wounds sustained by Monsieur Trobellec were similar to those that killed your friend."

"Wait a minute," Pippa said, standing up. "If you're accusing me of a double murder, I wish to have a lawyer present!" She gripped the table, shaking from stress and indignation. Why don't they throw in the murder of Madame Briand for good measure, she thought.

"Do you deny that you had an argument with Monsieur Trobellec?" the man asked.

"No comment," said Pippa. "I demand to have a lawyer present. I know my rights."

"Very well, Madame Sinclair," said Maguy. Her voice showed no emotion. "Do you have a lawyer?"

The only person Pippa knew was the notary. Maybe she could recommend somebody? But what were the chances of that on a Saturday night?

"No, I don't," she said.

"So we shall find you an *avocat d'office*," came the reply. Who knew how long it would take to find a duty solicitor so late, Pippa wondered. She knew that under French procedure she could be kept in a cell for twenty-four hours, which could be extended if justified. She was struggling not to cry. The one person who could help her was Yann, but she knew she had to keep him out of this.

"So am I being questioned as a suspect in this case?" she asked in a small voice.

"You are here in *audition libre*," Maguy said. "This is not a *garde à vue*—"

"Oh, really?" Pippa couldn't help but cut in. "It doesn't feel so voluntary from where I'm standing."

"But of course, Madame," Maguy said. "You may contact a member of your family if you wish."

But I don't have any family here! Pippa had never felt so alone. Her family was in England and she couldn't even ring Jennifer.

"Please wait here," the adjudant said, and the two gendarmes left the room.

Not knowing whether she was being filmed, Pippa opened her handbag and wiped the sweat from her face. It was going to be a long evening.

CHAPTER 38

It was almost midnight when Pippa left the gendarmerie, knowing that four hours later her alarm would wake her for another day's work.

She felt drained of all emotion. The second round of questioning in the presence of a duty lawyer had taken its toll.

Maguy Gallou had returned to the morning of Derek's death, probing her exact movements before she'd arrived at the house on the river. The gendarme obviously remembered how Pippa had seemed nervous, and indeed she also recalled her sweaty palms at the thought that she might be a suspect because of the breadcrumbs on the dead man's sweater.

Luckily the lawyer, who came dressed in jeans and a T-shirt, having had to interrupt a family dinner, had stepped in to point out that the line of questioning was circumstantial at best. The young man also said that as the details of Derek's death were in the public domain, Tristan Trobellec could have been the victim of a copycat murder. After exchanging a glance and consulting their notes, the two gendarmes allowed Pippa to go through her version once again.

As she sat in the back of a taxi on her way home, so tired she was almost light-headed, she remembered talking to Jennifer about Camus and *L'Étranger*. Meursault was found guilty because of his behaviour at his mother's funeral, she'd said, likening the situation to Solenn after Derek's death. But what about her own behaviour? No wonder the police thought she was guilty; she was already behaving as though she'd killed him when they'd shown up!

She felt impending disaster creeping towards her, despite the intervention of the friendly lawyer. They'd let her go, but she presumed that she could still be charged at any moment.

The taxi came to a halt outside her house. She paid the driver and turned her head towards Yann's house in case there was any sign he was still up. But of course he'd gone to bed. He was another early riser.

Her legs trembled slightly as they carried her up the drive to her front door. She was so weary that all she could do was put one foot in front of the other. She made her way upstairs and fell into a deep sleep. When the alarm went off, she awoke with a jump. It interrupted a nightmare in which she was facing a circular firing squad in her back garden, tied to one of her gladioli.

* * *

It was still dark when Pippa left the house for the bakery. The family across the road were safe asleep in their house. She reminded herself to call in on them after work in case they could corroborate her time of departure the previous morning, which would solidify her alibi. She couldn't be in two places at once, could she?

She gradually relaxed in the solitude of the early morning, spent baking the first batches of baguettes and croissants before she opened the shop at eight. The smell of freshly baked bread wafted through the bakery when the first customer opened the door.

She rang Jennifer from the back room as soon as she thought she would be up and around.

"This is incomprehensible!" Jennifer exclaimed. "I just don't understand why they'd call you in."

"It seems that somebody saw my car in Ploumenel at about the time Bucky was killed."

"Oh," said Jennifer. Pippa wondered what was going through her mind. But after a short pause, Jennifer continued, "But that's not possible, is it?"

"Of course not! Why would I go there when I was on my way to the market in Carhaix. Either the witness is lying or there's another red Mégane somewhere in the vicinity!"

"Hmm. I see. And is there anyone who could back you up?"

"I think my only chance is one of the neighbours, hopefully the family living opposite. But it might be a long shot," said Pippa. She heard the bakery door being pushed open. "I've got a customer, I've got to go."

"Sure. Let's talk later," said Jennifer. "Maybe this evening? I'm taking Mariam to her art class this afternoon. Let me think about this. But try not to worry."

* * *

The day dragged on at the bakery. Pippa began to wonder whether her customers were staying away because of the rumour mill.

She locked up as usual, after letting Gwen leave early, and trailed home. As she approached her house she noticed the children playing in the front garden opposite.

With her heart jumping from stress, Pippa greeted them and asked whether their parents were at home before ringing the doorbell.

Morgane answered. "Ah, *bonsoir*, Peeper. Are you in trouble again?"

Pippa couldn't help smiling. "I'm afraid I am . . ." She blurted out, "I'm embarrassed to tell you that last night I was taken in for questioning at the gendarmerie in connection with the death of the baker in Ploumenel, Monsieur Trobellec."

Her eyes wide, Morgane replied, "Oh, I'm sorry to hear that." She added, "Do come in. I've not done the washing up yet, but never mind."

She led the way along the hall to a kitchen identical to Pippa's. Noticing the stairs, Pippa asked, "Yours is a three-bedroom version, is it?"

"Yes, that's right. All the ones on this side of the street are. But do sit down. Would you like something to drink? My husband is watching TV in the living room so we can sit here."

"I'm fine, thanks. I don't want to put you to any trouble." Pippa drew up a chair and they both sat at the kitchen table. The faint odour of cooked fish hung in the air.

"I'm sorry, I'd offer you a biscuit, except that I don't have any time to bake any more," said Morgane. "But how can I help?"

"It's just that I was wondering whether you might have seen me leave yesterday morning, on my way to the market."

Morgane replied immediately, "Oh yes, of course. I saw you putting your loaves into the car when I went into the front room to pick up my daughter's cardigan."

"And do you know what time that was?"

"Let me see. I think it would have been about eight thirty. Yes, that's right, because the children had just come down for breakfast."

"Thank you," said Pippa, in a rush of gratitude. "Would you be prepared to confirm that to the gendarmes?"

Morgane frowned, as she hesitated. "Is it necessary? I will, of course, but is it important?"

"I'm afraid it's really important, because it confirms my version of events . . . if you don't mind. You see, it's to do with where I was at the moment when Tristan was killed. And I was actually about to leave home for the market." She shrugged. "I can't be in two places at once, can I?"

Morgane shook her head. She gave Pippa a sympathetic glance. "So you mean there's a witness who says you were at the Ploumenel bakery at the same time? That's weird."

"That person, whoever it is, is lying. But that's why I need someone to confirm what happened."

"Of course, Peeper. This must be very distressing for you."

Pippa felt a lump in her throat and was unable to speak for a moment. Instead she nodded, and then got up to go. "I've disturbed you enough. But thank you so much, Morgane, I'm so grateful."

Morgane accompanied her to the door and Pippa said goodbye to the children in the front. As an afterthought, she called out to Morgane, "The next time I bake some *galettes bretonnes*, I'll bring you over a batch."

She crossed the street. As she walked up her drive, Yann's car pulled in next door.

She opened her front door and heard footsteps on the drive, realising that he had got out of the car and was running after her. Quickly he came inside, pushing the door closed behind him, and they embraced.

"My dear Peeper, what is happening?"

She began to sob for the first time since her ordeal, and he held her close.

"Someone's trying to frame me, I'm telling you!" she exclaimed. "Your colleagues say they have a witness who saw my car outside Tristan's bakery yesterday morning at about the time of his death. But this is obviously a lie!"

Yann stroked the tears from her cheek and looked at her.

"This must be a mistake," he said.

"It's worse than a mistake, it's an out and out lie," she insisted. "Can't you find out where it came from?"

He frowned before replying quietly, "You know I can't do that. I cannot be involved in this case because of you. But I know you have done nothing. I am here to support you." He hugged her again. Of course he couldn't help, she realised, remembering the vicious rumours that she was already a police informer because of their relationship.

"Thank you," she said. "That means a lot. Luckily the neighbours here have said they'll confirm the time that I left home yesterday for the market."

"That's good," he said. "Everything will be fine, I'm sure. I came home on my break because I knew you would be back," he added. "But now I have to return to work."

CHAPTER 39

Jennifer and Mariam arrived in Ploumenel at two o'clock sharp that same afternoon.

But there was no car in the driveway and no response when they knocked on the front door. They were about to leave when Louise opened the door.

"I'm so sorry. I did hear you but I was on the phone to Madeleine," she explained. "What a day I've had! The police have been here since yesterday, interviewing everybody in the village."

Without being asked for an explanation, she went on, "Isn't this awful? Do you know I was the one who found Tristan on the floor yesterday, but it was too late to help him!"

With a quick glance at Mariam to spare her any pain, Jennifer replied, "I'm so sorry."

"And Madeleine is devastated, of course," said Louise. "Come in, let me take Mariam through to the studio."

"Are you sure you're up to it? We can come back another time," Jennifer began, to Mariam's obvious dismay. But Louise insisted.

"No. It's fine." She turned to Mariam and said, "But why don't you go and wait for me there, the door's open, and I'll join you in a moment."

Mariam immediately set off, carrying her painting equipment.

"So I'll come back in a couple of hours to pick her up?" said Jennifer.

"Absolutely." Louise had a faraway look in her eyes.

"Are you sure you're alright?" Jennifer asked.

"As alright as I can be after finding a dead body!" came the reply, half laugh, half cry.

"Is Tegwenn not in?"

Louise shook her head. "Not at the moment, no. He had an errand in Louennec, he said."

Jennifer hesitated before asking, "So do you want to tell me about it?"

Louise sighed. "Do you remember me saying that I was doing a portrait of Madeleine? Well, yesterday morning, I knew that she'd be at the bakery with Tristan getting ready for market. But when I got there she wasn't around, and that's when I found him in the back room. I called Madeleine straight away, of course, but she was already on her way to the market. He must have been killed after she left."

"We noticed that there was nobody at their stall yesterday. I suppose she was too upset," said Jennifer.

"Yes. She told me she'd go straight home after returning to the bakery. I suppose the police must have already been at the shop when Madeleine got back."

"They took her in for questioning!" Louise added. "Can you believe it?"

Jennifer shook her head sorrowfully. "Who would do such a thing?"

"I understand they're looking for the murder weapon. The bakery is a crime scene! It would be funny if it wasn't so sad," said Louise.

"Well, I suppose they're only doing their job," Jennifer remarked. "Look, I'd better let you get on with your day. I'll see you in a bit."

Jennifer returned to her car and decided to take a detour round the village on her way home. She was burning with curiosity to see the bakery with police tape around it. But the car was brought to a halt by a group of gendarmes standing by a bridge over the stream. They were talking to three teenagers, who were pointing to the stream and talking animatedly, all of them speaking at the same time, or interrupting one another.

She parked on the verge and went to the bank. She could see a gendarme standing in the stream up to his knees, and a feeding frenzy going on in front of him. Had the kids been feeding the trout? It wasn't a crime, she thought.

As though on cue, a trout flew out of the river before sinking into the water again. The gendarme was bent over, obviously trying to find something. She waited, wondering what was going on. He seemed to be pushing fish aside in his search.

After a couple more minutes, he stood up, holding a metal rod, which had a sodden piece of bread stuck to one end. Jennifer instinctively grabbed her camera and took a picture of the gendarme, his hand in a glove.

"*Et voilà!*" he shouted to his colleagues, with a triumphant smile.

CHAPTER 40

When Jennifer returned to Louise's cottage, Mariam was waiting for her in the front room, ready to leave.

"Everything OK?" Jennifer asked.

"Yeah. It's great. We're doing portraits. Today I did a self-portrait."

"A self-portrait? That sounds difficult. Let me see . . ."

"I'll show you when we get home," said Mariam. They drove along empty lanes, scattered with dead leaves, past the towering wind farm turbines overlooking Louennec that Jennifer hated.

White clouds as puffy as whipped cream hung over the house, where Byron was standing guard by the front door. He gave a long howl of recognition as they pulled up, causing Luke and his friend Alain to appear from along the grassy track to check that all was well.

Mariam opened her backpack as soon as they went into the kitchen. She clearly wanted to show Jennifer her work. Carefully, she took out a file containing a sheet of paper.

"OK, let's have a look," said Jennifer, taking it. The drawing closely resembled Mariam, with her almond eyes, sulky lips and snub nose. She'd conveyed the thickness of her wavy hair.

The girl's eyes were looking to one side, not directly at the viewer.

"This is fantastic. I'd recognise you immediately," she said. "Well done."

Mariam, for once, accepted the compliment, pleased with the result.

"And did Louise give you any tips?"

"Yes, of course. It was quite scientific. She had me draw lines across my face on the paper. And she made me use a mirror. It was weird, studying myself." She grinned. "Louise said that next time she'd let me try to do one of Madeleine from photos. She's done a lot of pictures of her."

* * *

Jennifer found herself thinking about Pippa as she roasted some vegetables in the oven and took out some slices of ham for everyone except Mariam. Philippe wasn't around as he had an early morning market the next day.

After doing the washing up she told them that she had to visit Pippa and persuaded Luke and his friend to shut in the animals, which had become one of their favourite tasks. Mariam insisted that she was fine on her own upstairs.

It was dark by the time she arrived at Pippa's and found her finishing a chunk of Camembert with a glass of red wine.

"Do you want some *vino collapso*?" Pippa asked. "I'm afraid I needed it tonight. I'm not sure I'll be very good company."

"Sure, give me a glass," said Jennifer, pulling up a chair. "But wait till you hear this . . . I was in Ploumenel when the cops found the murder weapon that killed Bucky!"

"What? Wow!"

"Yes, it was a metal rod, apparently inside a baguette, just like what was used to kill Derek." Jennifer quickly told her about her encounter on the bridge. "It's bound to be all over the paper tomorrow." She took a long sip of her wine before adding: "Have you got some paper handy? Let's draw up a list..."

"What sort of a list?" Pippa asked, genuinely puzzled. She got up and searched for paper and pens.

"Suspects!" said Jennifer. "These two murders are linked, aren't they? It's obvious from what I saw today."

"Do you think so? I suppose it makes sense. The gendarmes seemed to think the head injuries were similar."

Pippa came back to the table and handed a sheet of paper to Jennifer.

"Right. What have these two murders got in common?" Jennifer asked.

"Me!" said Pippa, before letting out a nervous laugh.

"Apart from you, I mean. Unless you're planning on handing yourself in," said Jennifer.

"I feel like I almost did." Pippa hung her head, looking sideways across the table at her friend.

"Stop beating yourself up, will you? We're taking as a given that it wasn't you."

"OK. What I want to know is who lied about my car being in the village. And how the gendarmes knew about me having a dispute with Bucky," said Pippa. As she spoke, she suddenly remembered something.

"Wait — I know!" she went on. "Madeleine knew about the row with him, because she was there when I went over and tore him off a strip. It must have been her, because Bucky never filed an official complaint to the gendarmerie after accusing me of sabotaging his electricity supply. So unless Yann said something, which I doubt, none of his colleagues would know."

"Thank you." Jennifer wrote down Madeleine's name in capitals. "I found out today from Mariam's art teacher that the gendarmes have been questioning everyone in Ploumenel, and that Madeleine was taken in. They let her out though, so she's obviously been ruled out."

"Ah. Like me then."

"Yes, exactly. So, like I keep telling you, you don't need to worry. However, what about the car?"

"Maybe that was Madeleine too," Pippa suggested. "She might have noticed the colour of my car when she saw me that day. I parked right outside the bakery."

"OK. So we'll put a question mark after Madeleine. Although I suppose that the gendarmes let her go because she didn't have a motive. And we don't have a connection to Derek. Do you think she's been pretending to like us all this time? It strikes me that she's probably not a fan because her husband didn't like you."

Pippa frowned and rubbed her chin while she considered Jennifer's theory. "Fair enough, I suppose. So she might be trying to implicate me, just like Sylvie tried to implicate me in Madame Briand's death."

"Quite possibly." Jennifer sucked the end of the biro as she thought. "You've not been murdered though, have you?"

After a few moments she wrote down Solenn, again in capitals.

"Solenn? Are you mad?" Pippa asked. "Why would she have knocked off her husband?"

"It happens, doesn't it? And do you remember us talking about Solenn's open marriage? I'm convinced that maybe these two murders are connected."

"Yes. I agree about that, but I really think we should rule out Solenn. I just don't see her as a killer," said Pippa.

"OK. But there's definitely something fishy going on with Louise, who doesn't seem to like her," said Jennifer.

"But that's because of Solenn and Tegwenn being an item, don't you think? And what about him?" Pippa interjected. "Maybe Solenn plotted with Tegwenn, who wielded the baguette!"

Jennifer wrote down his name as well, before looking at the list.

"Right. Louise is good friends with Madeleine," she added, drawing a line linking the two names. "But I can't see why Tegwenn would kill Bucky. Derek, maybe, but not Bucky.

"Anyone else?" she said. "Has Yann given you any deep background?"

Pippa shook her head vigorously. "He can't and he won't," she stressed. "Another drink?" she asked, picking up the wine bottle.

"Just a drop, I'm driving," said Jennifer, raising her glass for the refill. "And the kids are on their own.

"Wait," she added. "I've just remembered something. Do you know what Jonathan told me about their open marriage? He heard from Derek that he'd been seeing a hairdresser from Carhaix and someone from one of the villages. So *if* it was one of these two, we assume that the murderer was a woman."

"That's a big *if*," said Pippa. "But now we know the hairdresser's identity. And wait, what if the other woman's village is Ploumenel?" Pippa mused. "That could put Louise in the frame, which is why she reacted like she did when you mentioned Solenn? Maybe she wanted Derek to herself?"

Jennifer dutifully wrote down Louise, but was dubious. "Hang on, I still don't get why she'd kill Bucky though."

"Obviously because Louise is Madeleine's lover too and they decided to knock him off!" said Pippa.

"Are you serious?" said Jennifer. "This is getting out of hand."

She looked down again at the list of names, shaking her head. "It's true that it could be Ploumenel. Jonathan said Derek's other mistress might be from Kerivac, but he said himself he couldn't remember what he'd been told by Derek."

She rested her elbows on the table and stared again at the names. "But I'll tell you what. It looks to me like in both cases the victim knew the killer. For example, the murderer came in through the back door at Derek's . . . and I presume that he or she would have known exactly where to find Bucky on a Saturday morning."

"Hmm," said Pippa. "I guess quite a few people would know he'd be getting his bread ready for market . . . But how could it be the same person with that knowledge in both cases? Where is Yann when we need him?"

Jennifer stretched out her hand across the table, and squeezed Pippa's arm. "If Yann can't help, it's down to us then, isn't it?"

CHAPTER 41

The headline in *Le Télégramme* said it all: "*Double meurtre dans le Finistère*".

Jennifer had returned from the school run and spread out the paper on the kitchen table. The story explained that, as she and Pippa had suspected, it was a double murder because Bucky, like Derek, had been killed with a metal rod stuffed inside a baguette.

The photo illustrating the story was hers. What a stroke of luck that had been, she thought. The murder weapon had been cast into the stream and then spotted by children who had wanted to break up the bread to feed the trout which congregated under the bridge, according to the paper.

Jennifer picked up the phone and rang Pippa, who was at the bakery even on her day off. "They used my pic!"

"Congratulations," said Pippa. "So we were right about it being the same person."

"Unless it was a copycat crime. But I'm going to get out my list and have another look," said Jennifer.

"OK," said Pippa, before ringing off.

Jennifer put the kettle on and made herself a cup of tea. She went looking for the sheet of paper containing the list of names from the previous evening and scrutinised it. She couldn't imagine why the same person would have a grudge against both Derek and Bucky that would cause him or her to kill both of them.

Derek was killed first, she thought, therefore maybe something had happened subsequently that had prompted the second murder. But what?

She checked the time. She had to drop off some photos in Carhaix for the paper, and she wondered whether she'd have time to have lunch there before returning home to do some gardening. *Why not see whether Solenn was free?*

* * *

Solenn left the dentist's surgery at exactly one o'clock and gave Jennifer a smile. As usual Jennifer felt dowdy in her shabby jeans compared to Solenn's smart attire and careful make-up.

"I only have an hour," Solenn warned. "Where shall we go?"

"Maybe the pizzeria by the town hall?" Jennifer suggested. They strolled along the main road, past the mediaeval tourism office to Les Bonnets Rouges pizzeria which was already busy.

"Is this OK for you?" Jennifer asked, suddenly unsure of what she was doing.

They were ushered to a table in the corner. Solenn suggested sharing a single pizza between them.

"I'm trying not to eat too much comfort food," she said, smoothing down her trousers. Jennifer would have been happy to be anything near Solenn's weight.

"Maybe share a salad as well?" she offered. "It won't kill us."

They ordered their food and sipped glasses of water from a carafe while they waited.

"What did you want to see me about?" Solenn asked. "The history of the *bonnets rouges*?"

Jennifer hadn't given any thought to the name of the restaurant until Solenn quickly explained that it referred originally to the Breton nationalists who had first risen up against Louis XIV's taxes. In recent years they'd put on their red caps again, led by the mayor of Carhaix, in protest against a green tax on road freight.

"So we are revolutionaries here," she said with a smile.

"Oh, I've noticed that," said Jennifer. "Although even we Brits have sometimes revolted too. When I was growing up there was rioting across the country against what Margaret Thatcher called a poll tax."

"And what happened?" Solenn asked.

"Well, looking back, it led to Thatcher's resignation."

Solenn raised her eyebrows. "So Britons and Bretons have something in common," she said. "Revolution!"

Looking across at Solenn, with her pearl necklace and matching earrings, Jennifer couldn't think of a less likely revolutionary.

She cleared her throat and began. "Anyway, what I wanted to mention was that Pippa was called in to be interviewed at the gendarmerie after Tristan was killed.

"I want to help her as she's very upset. I don't know whether you saw the paper but they think that it's the same person who killed Derek and Buck— Tristan," she said, correcting herself swiftly.

"Yes, I did see that article. But I don't understand how it could be the same person," said Solenn.

"I think it comes down to connections," said Jennifer. "Assuming that the killer is local, I'm sure that if we break down the circles that you and Derek, and Tristan and Madeleine moved in, there would be at least one person who might have had a motive to kill them both. Do you see what I mean?"

The waiter brought their pizza and Solenn cut it into quarters before replying. She picked up a slice dripping with mozzarella and squeezed the tip into her tiny mouth.

"*Tu crois?*" she said. "Don't you think that the police would be making their own connections? I don't see why we need to get involved. Although I'm not very impressed by their progress, I must say. I thought they would have made an arrest by now."

"But that's the point," Jennifer said, watching Solenn chew. "We know our networks so much better than they do. And excuse me for asking, but I'm wondering whether there might be any crossover of Derek's clients and your lovers. Or possibly his, I don't know. But you're the only person who might be aware of that."

Solenn gave Jennifer a long stare, prompting her to add, "I'm sorry to ask you this. It's obviously none of my business—" Solenn nodded — "but I'm only trying to help."

It was Jennifer's turn to pick up a slice of her Four Seasons, and she chose the quarter with mushrooms. Unfortunately they dropped off her slice onto the plate just as she picked it up. She wished that she'd used a knife and fork but it was too late now. She wiped her chin with a napkin.

"Can't Pippa's gendarme friend help?" Solenn inquired drily. Jennifer was starting to regret ever getting in touch with her.

"Actually no. He's not involved in the investigation and naturally doesn't want to get involved for professional reasons," Jennifer replied. At least Solenn seemed to understand the position.

Solenn took a deep breath and said, "As you know, Derek and I didn't talk about our relationships. It would have been too messy, and also we didn't want each other to get jealous."

Jennifer nodded, wiping her hands on a paper napkin. This lunch was obviously not going to produce any breakthrough, she thought. But what was Solenn hiding? Surely she wanted Derek's murderer to be identified. She studied Solenn's oval face, which gave nothing away. She remembered Pippa's earlier hypothesis about Solenn. Could she have . . . ?

How well did she know Solenn anyway? In reality, she realised, the Frenchwoman had always been an extension of their friend Derek, with whom they'd had much more in common, including his playfulness and love of pantomime. But she still didn't see her as a murderer.

Solenn broke into her train of thought. "But as for his client list, I gave a copy to the gendarmerie and I don't mind sharing it with you, if you think it might shed light on your theory about *connections*," she said. Then she added: "Shall we get the bill? I'd better get back to work."

Jennifer looked down at the untidy remains of their pizza, whose crusts decorated the edge of the plate, and turned round to find the waiter. At least she'd managed to coax Solenn into cooperating. But what was Solenn's strategy, she wondered. To hand over a minimum of information while keeping her secrets to herself?

At this point, Jennifer thought, she had nothing to lose.

"By the way," she asked, "was your hairdresser one of Derek's fitness customers?"

"My hairdresser?"

"Yes, your friend Annick. You remember, you introduced us at the *méchoui*."

"Ah. Yes, Annick. Yes she was." Solenn frowned as though she didn't see the connection.

"Does she live in Carhaix?"

"No. Kerivac." Solenn looked up as the waiter was standing by her side with the payment machine.

"What are you trying to prove, Jennifer?" she said, with a menacing tone in her voice.

"You're sharing the bill?" the waiter asked. "That will be eleven euros each."

CHAPTER 42

Ever since starting her new life as a baker, Pippa had listened to local radio after being woken by the alarm.

She found that the news fed her conversations with customers throughout the day. Usually, while draining a large bowl of strong coffee and eating toasted baguette with marmalade, she only listened with half an ear. But that morning she was jolted into full consciousness when the presenter mentioned Louennec.

A woman had been arrested for the murder of a local dignitary. Had there been another murder? she thought with alarm. She hadn't seen Yann for days, and she feared he was avoiding her. Then she remembered that Madame Briand had been described as a pillar of the community by the priest at her funeral. She switched up the volume and heard that it was Madame Briand's carer who had been arrested.

She sat back with satisfaction that she'd been right after all. She felt like punching the air, because the arrest was bound to lay to rest all the horrible rumours swirling around her. Sylvie Le Goff had better watch out, she thought. She wanted to know more, but the radio presenter had already moved on to the subject of another outbreak of avian flu.

She went to work a few minutes later with a spring in her step, glancing at Yann's car parked in his drive as she left the house. She was still disappointed that he'd said nothing to her, and that another day had gone by without them seeing each other. He knew how affected she'd been by the groundless accusations flung at her. But by the time she reached the bakery, her good humour had been restored and she got to work in the back with the radio on loud.

Pippa wondered whether Jennifer knew about the carer. Surely she would have told her if so. She waited until Gwen had arrived, and she knew that Jennifer would be back from the school run, before calling her.

"Wait a sec," said Jennifer on learning the news. "Let me check if there's anything in the paper."

Pippa heard her footsteps on the stone floor and the click of the front door. A few moments later, the door slammed shut and Jennifer came back on the line.

"Let's see," she said, shuffling through the pages. "Here we are. It's the top story on the Louennec page, of course."

"Does it say anything about how they caught the carer?"

"I can't say it does, no. It just says she confessed. She was Portuguese, was she?"

"Yes, that's right."

"It says she confessed to poisoning her," said Jennifer. "It was mushrooms! Wow. So it wasn't a baguette murder after all."

Pippa smiled to herself. She was vindicated.

"Actually, I was going to invite you over tonight or tomorrow," Jennifer went on. She explained that she'd seen Solenn a couple of days earlier and was waiting to receive the list of Derek's fitness clients from her.

"She also said that her hairdresser went to Derek's classes, and that she lives in Kerivac. So I think Jonathan got confused. I'm not sure whether it's significant but anyway, as soon as Solenn's email drops, I'll let you know, and we can take it from there," said Jennifer. "Sound good?"

"Sure. Great. I've no plans this week."

"Really?" Jennifer asked, picking up on Pippa's tone of voice. "Everything OK?"

"Yes, don't worry," Pippa said hurriedly.

She rang off and returned to the counter where Gwen was serving a customer. She wondered how many of them would have heard about Madame Briand's carer and made the connection with the poison pen writer. That was all water under the bridge now, she thought.

***

That evening, when Pippa walked home, she noticed that Yann's car was in his drive. She hesitated, not knowing how he would react if she appeared at his front door. They'd never been in a situation like this, with no arrangement to see each other in the future.

The whole thing about her injecting herself into investigations had maybe cast a shadow over their relationship. He'd warned her more than once, hadn't he, about being discreet? She'd started to think that he'd never be in touch about seeing her again.

She sighed. She missed him. She missed his gentle teasing, his cooking, and his warm embrace. But she definitely wasn't going to go crawling back if he'd decided that their relationship was over. Or was it? She was still debating whether to go round to his house regardless when his front door opened and he waved as though nothing had happened.

"*Bonsoir*, Peeper!" he said. "*Ca va?*" He gestured as though inviting her in. "*Tu rentres?*"

Pippa had half a mind to decline his invitation, but grinned and walked round the box hedge to his door. He shut the door behind her and they kissed. Maybe she'd been worrying about nothing, she thought.

"I'm sorry," he said. "I felt I had to leave you alone with all this situation."

He waved his arm as though indicating that whatever the situation was, it was too big for both of them.

"I know. I understand," she said. "But why didn't you tell me about Madame Briand's carer?"

"Because, Peeper, I didn't want this to be traced to you at all. You told me that some of the people in the village think that you are passing on information to me. That's why."

So that was it. Yann was just being cautious. Or over-cautious. She couldn't blame him for that. He'd wanted to protect her.

"I see. Thank you for telling me," she said. "But now can you tell me how come she confessed?"

Yann broke into a wide smile. "It's thanks to you," he said. "Monsieur le curé came round to see me about something he'd heard from Madame Briand. We also spoke to the notary, which gave us enough to pay a visit to the carer. Once we told her that we knew that Madame Briand had changed her will in her favour only days before her death, she told us everything. She had mixed death cap mushrooms into a risotto the day before she died."

Death cap mushrooms!

"I wonder whether *le corbeau* knew about the mushrooms when they sent me the letter?" said Pippa. She was starting to wonder whether the carer herself might have tried to deflect attention by accusing Pippa.

"Maybe, maybe not," said Yann. Pippa frowned. "I'm sorry, Peeper, but I don't think we'll ever find out. But we do have the murderer."

CHAPTER 43

Jennifer pulled out a folded sheet of paper from her jeans and smoothed it out on the table.

She and Pippa were seated at the Central Café after wrapping up their market stalls for the day.

"I'm sorry this took so long," Jennifer said, "but I had to remind Solenn about this before she emailed it to me last night."

"Hmm. Interesting," said Pippa. "She's not exactly falling over herself to help, is she?"

"Anyway, we've got it now. Never mind," said Jennifer. They both sat back while the waiter placed their coffees in front of them. Jennifer caught Philippe's eye; he was standing at the bar with Jean-Luc enjoying their glass of red wine. Some things never change, she thought.

"Everything OK with you?" she asked Pippa.

"Much better, now that Yann is talking to me again," came the reply.

Jennifer patted her on the hand. "I knew it would turn out fine in the end," she said with a smile.

"And you?" Pippa asked.

"Things are great with Philippe, yes. Mariam is doing well at her art class, so that's a load off my mind. Luke is just as bubbly as usual, and that leaves Jonathan, who's moved into his own place but is still behaving like a jerk."

They turned their attention to the typed list of names, which looked like a timetable. Derek seemed to be running two classes per week, possibly for different levels of fitness. The one that caught their attention was the Tuesday one — the day that he died.

Pippa ran her finger down the names. "There aren't very many. A dirty dozen. That narrows it down," she said. "And maybe fewer of them for the first class after the *rentrée*."

"Do you see Gabriel there?" Jennifer asked. "He's the guy who was at the funeral and who seems to be pretty close to Solenn these days."

"Do you think he's definitely her lover? Isn't he a bit old?"

"He's older than her, yes, but so was Derek," said Jennifer.

"True," said Pippa. "But if you're suggesting that he might have a motive for knocking off his rival, Derek, we don't have anything to connect him with Bucky. Of course there might be two killers on the loose . . ."

"Hmm." Jennifer put an elbow on the table and gave the impression of thinking carefully. "But if it was two killers, wouldn't they use different methods?"

Pippa was still examining the client list. "Oh look, there's Christine. I hope the police interviewed her. She's in cahoots with the dreaded Sylvie. And there's Annick, the hairdresser, who we think was another squeeze of Derek."

"Yes, but neither of them have a connection to both victims, do they?" said Jennifer.

"Christine does. She knew Bucky, obviously, through Madeleine, and they're neighbours in Ploumenel."

She'd reached the bottom of the list.

"Oh dear," she said. "Look who's here."

"Who?"

"It's Madeleine."

CHAPTER 44

"Hang on," said Jennifer.

"Hang on, what? It's obvious from this list that Madeleine is somebody who is connected to Derek and also to Bucky, the two dead people in the *commune*!" said Pippa.

"Yes. But we don't know what the connection was, do we? And I don't suppose she'd tell us. So we need to find out more before jumping to conclusions," said Jennifer.

"And she's a baker . . ." said Pippa. "I would remind you about the breadcrumbs on both bodies."

"So are you, and you have connections with both Derek and Bucky, but you're not the murderer . . ." Jennifer grinned. "What we need is a motive. Is it too early to mention this to Yann? Maybe the gendarmes have their own suspicions."

Pippa groaned. "Oh no. Much too soon. He'd wonder why I'm interfering again, just after we've made up."

"And let's face it, the second killing might have been a copycat murder. Maybe the cops said too much to the press about the metal rod in the baguette in the first place, which gave Bucky's killer the idea . . ."

"Look. We're going nowhere with this," said Pippa. "Let me get the bill and we'll think about it some more."

* * *

The next day it was Jonathan's turn to take Mariam to her art lesson, which he did with typically bad grace.

"Look, if you're busy, I can pick her up afterwards," Jennifer offered, although she wondered why he never had time on a Sunday afternoon. Why was he playing so much golf? Surely he hadn't got another girlfriend already? But what if he had? She no longer cared, as long as his parental duties didn't suffer.

"Thank you," he said, getting into the car with Mariam. "I've got golf this afternoon."

Jennifer frowned and — followed by Byron — walked along to the market garden where Philippe was picking apples.

"I'm going to pick up Mariam in two hours," she said with a smile. "But I'm free until then."

"What about Luke?" he asked. "Is he around?"

"He cycled off to see Alain after lunch," she said.

"Perfect," he smiled. They went back to the house arm in arm, watched by Byron, who sank to the ground assuming his guard dog position outside the front door.

* * *

When Jennifer showed up at Louise's house to collect Mariam, there was no sign of anyone inside. She rang the doorbell and waited until someone came out of the barn.

Louise appeared, wiping her hands on a paint-covered apron.

"I'm so sorry. We're just finishing up," she said, threading her way through the living room.

"Is everything alright?"

Louise stopped in her tracks. "Yes. Fine. But I did want to ask you something. We've been working from photos, you see."

Jennifer waited for the explanation, and Louise continued, "Which country is Mariam from, originally?"

Jennifer hadn't expected the question, but replied, "Somalia."

Louise nodded. "Ah yes. I see. I knew it must be a Muslim country. It's just that she brought in some photos of women in robes and started talking about her birth mother. I suppose that would make sense to you."

Jennifer ground her teeth. She didn't want to have this conversation with a stranger.

"Did she say anything in particular?"

"She said that she'd been born in a refugee camp, and that she wanted to find her mother. She sounded quite excited about it. I suppose at that age, adopted children are curious about their origins."

"Yes. Quite," said Jennifer. "And her drawing?"

"Oh. Yes. She's really into it. She has a natural talent. After these portraits, we're going to move into landscapes. Shall we see how she's getting on?"

Jennifer followed Louise into the barn where Mariam was standing at the far end near a big window. She was studying a drawing pinned to the easel, her pencil poised. Jennifer approached and could see a mosque in the background.

"Do you mind, Jennifer? There's just one more thing that I want to show Mariam," said Louise.

"Of course."

The teacher reached out and began demonstrating a pencil technique to Mariam, leaving Jennifer to look round the art that was propped up along the walls. Jennifer went over to the series of portraits of Madeleine, and began inspecting each one. They'd obviously been done over a period of years. She noticed that Louise had almost finished the large one showing her kneading bread in the bakery's back room in her apron. She'd added fresh details which showed Madeleine wearing plastic gloves for the operation, and cracks on the dark wall behind her next to the proofing chamber.

Jennifer was standing next to a desk where there was a pile of photos. Again, she recognised Madeleine. These must be the snaps that Louise had mentioned earlier, she thought. She checked that Louise was still otherwise occupied, and started to look through them.

One was a group photo, which Jennifer realised must be of the local villagers. It showed Louise and Madeleine linking arms with a woman wearing glasses holding a terrier on a leash. Jennifer couldn't be sure but the woman resembled Christine. Tegwenn stood in the background with his arms around Louise and Madeleine. Was it Bucky who had taken the photo?

In others, Madeleine was variously shown shaping bread — obviously in the back room of the bakery — and strolling on the beach with Bucky. In another, she was standing on a stone bridge crossing a stream. A man had an arm round her. Jennifer was struck because of the implied intimacy and by the fact that the man was not her husband. Who had taken the picture? Was it Louise? She looked more closely. It seemed to be recent, although there was nothing to indicate a date.

She gasped inwardly when she saw that the person with his arm round Madeleine was Derek.

CHAPTER 45

Jennifer dropped the photo as if it was on fire.

Mariam and Louise still had their backs to her, engrossed in their artistry. Should she keep it as evidence? She had recognised the bridge where Derek and Madeleine were posing. It was the one in Ploumenel that she'd photographed the other day.

She looked down at the photo again as she debated whether to slip it into her bag. Would Louise notice? After all, it wasn't her property, that would be theft.

At that moment, Louise stepped back from the drawing and turned towards Jennifer.

"Is everything OK, Jennifer? You look as though you've seen a ghost."

"Oh yes, no, I was just looking at these portraits. You've certainly got Madeleine down to a T," she said.

"We've known each other a long time," said Louise. "She holds no secrets for me."

Really? But Jennifer held back.

"May I see Mariam's work? Is it finished?"

"I think so," said Louise. She turned to Mariam. "You've been very productive today. Well done."

Mariam cast her eyes to the ground at the compliment before stepping back so that her mother could get closer. She'd drawn a market scene in front of the mosque where veiled women had gathered. But one woman in the foreground was drawn in exquisite detail, her face resembling Mariam's.

Jennifer looked more closely at the picture, admiring the portrayal of vegetables and trinkets piled high on the stalls.

"This is really good," she said.

"Yes," said Louise. "I was suggesting that she might like to use a wash over the pencil, which would inject some colour, particularly into the mother figure."

The mother figure? Jennifer felt a stab of jealousy about the relationship between Mariam and Louise. How much had her daughter confided in the woman?

She kicked herself for her reaction. Why shouldn't Mariam confide in another adult? It was a sign that she was opening up, surely.

"Mariam has been exploring her background, you know. This is what the drawings are all about, isn't that right, Mariam?" Jennifer said.

"Yeah," came the answer.

Then Jennifer added, "In fact, she's now collecting money to send to Somalis in a big refugee camp in Kenya. We think it's the one where her biological mother took her when she escaped the civil war."

Had she shared too much, she wondered, with a quick glance at Mariam. But she didn't seem to mind. She was smiling.

"Oh how sweet," said Louise. "Let me get my purse."

Now Jennifer was embarrassed. "Oh, I didn't mean . . ." she stammered.

But Louise was already making her way back into the house. Jennifer and Mariam followed her. By the time they reached the sitting room, Louise had already got ten euros together in small change.

"Here you are," she said. Mariam held out her hand and thanked Louise profusely.

"Come on, Mariam, we'd better get home. We don't want to hold Louise up, do we?"

* * *

That evening, Jennifer waited until the children were upstairs and Philippe had returned home before picking up the phone to call Pippa about the photos. She knew instinctively that she'd have the best idea how to proceed.

"You see, I think that the one with Madeleine and Derek contains the answer to the riddle," she told Pippa.

"I agree. Or at least a possible solution to the riddle. But don't we need to get hold of it? Or at least manage to take a photo if we don't want to steal it," said Pippa. "I reckon we should go round. Then we can pass it on to Yann. It could be the proof the police are looking for."

Jennifer had feared as much. Pippa had a reckless side that she always flinched from.

"What's the hurry?" said Jennifer. "Next time I go round I can try and find it in the studio. Although we'd have to wait two weeks because it's Jonathan's turn to take Mariam next Sunday."

Pippa jumped in, saying, "Right, it's obvious. If we wait any longer, Louise will have a chance to tidy up the place. Did she notice you looking at it?"

Jennifer wrinkled her nose. "I'm not sure. Maybe. She said I looked as though I'd seen a ghost."

Pippa laughed. "And you had! It was Derek! So what if she was the one who took the photo? She must have known about them . . ."

"But are you suggesting we ask Louise for the photo?" Jennifer was starting to get nervous.

"Nope," said Pippa. "I'm suggesting that we sneak in to get it tonight."

CHAPTER 46

Jennifer rang off and was immediately struck by a sense of panic. Why had she agreed to this? They'd been lucky to get away with similar searches in the past, but to try to get into Louise's studio in darkness was another thing altogether.

What if the barn was alarmed? And of course it would be locked, she thought, even though she'd noticed that Louise seemed to keep it open. And what if Louise and Tegwenn had a guard dog? She had to admit that she'd never seen a dog on the property, only the cat. But still she wasn't convinced by Pippa's plan.

She wondered about asking Philippe to join them, in case of trouble. But then she decided that wouldn't be fair on him, even if he agreed to it.

A few minutes later she went upstairs and knocked on Mariam's door.

"What are you doing?" she asked.

Mariam turned round from her computer.

"Homework. I've got *exams* this year," she said, pointedly. "I'm learning all about how the French government wants to keep bee-killing pesticides."

"Are you sure? I thought they'd backed down on that after the EU court ruling."

"Keep up, Mum," said Mariam, suddenly wanting to explain the finer points of beet farmers and policy exemptions, which made Jennifer's eyes glaze over.

"Good. I have to go over to Pippa's for a bit. Probably no more than an hour, if that. Could you just . . ."

"Keep an eye on Luke?" Mariam finished the sentence for her.

Jennifer smiled. "Yes. Is that OK?"

"Sure. Have a nice time." Mariam turned back to her work, and Jennifer felt dismissed from the classroom.

* * *

Jennifer scanned the fields and hedges as Pippa drove along the darkened lanes. She didn't know what she was looking for, but didn't want to be taken by surprise.

"Are you sure you don't want to ask Louise straight out?" she asked Pippa.

"The gendarmes can do that, can't they? What we need is the proof that leads to Madeleine," said Pippa.

They reached Ploumenel and parked on a grassy verge at the entrance to the village before heading on foot to Louise's cottage.

"Maybe we should have gone later," said Jennifer. "I mean after they've gone to bed."

"I thought of that," said Pippa. "But it's possible that the upstairs bedroom overlooks the studio and they might hear us."

"Ah yes, you're right, with a bit of luck they'll be watching the telly in the front room," said Jennifer. But her stomach was still twisting with anxiety.

"One more thing," she added. "We need to think this through. What if they're not in the front room? They might be in the kitchen having dinner, and that room looks over the courtyard leading to the studio."

"Don't be such a wet blanket, we'll find out when we get there, won't we?"

Jennifer bristled at the description and didn't reply. They stood outside the cottage where a light hung over the front porch. Through the curtains they could see that the sitting room light was on. But there was no car in the driveway.

Pippa nudged Jennifer. "Somebody's in," she said. "Come on. Can we get round the side to the back?"

Jennifer had no idea. "I suppose so," she said, hanging back as Pippa strode on. They slid round the side of the house to the back where the cobbled courtyard led to the barn.

Jennifer began creeping forward in an exaggerated manner, which made Pippa burst out laughing.

"Shush!" said Jennifer. "We don't want anyone to hear us!"

She reached the wide barn door and turned the handle. It wasn't locked. With a glance at Pippa behind her, she pushed it open.

"Use your phone torch, don't switch on the light," Pippa said in a stage whisper. "I'll stand guard here."

They went inside and closed the door behind them. Pippa stood by the wall next to the door. Jennifer's phone illuminated the paintings by the wall in a thin arc of light. She walked on, her heart pounding, looking for the pile of photos on the desk near the Madeleine portraits.

"Damn," she said. "She's put them away somewhere." She flashed the phone torch over nearby surfaces but there were no photos to be seen. Maybe in a drawer? She opened the desk drawers one by one and shone the light inside. There were files containing photos which she quickly flipped through. But she couldn't find what she was looking for. She saw a cupboard by the wall and quickly inspected the contents.

"It's all her painting equipment. Where the hell has she put those photos?"

A door slammed in the house, so loudly that they both jumped.

"Can you hear voices?" Pippa said. "It sounds like they're in the kitchen."

Jennifer stood still to listen. The kitchen window must be open because she could clearly hear the raised voices from the back of the barn. Louise was shouting, presumably at Tegwenn who must have just returned.

"I know where you've been!" she said. "*J'en ai marre!* I've had enough! I know all about your girlfriend, you liar!"

Jennifer felt a pang of guilt as she remembered her fraught conversations with Jonathan when he had denied that he was in a relationship with Emma. It was embarrassing to think that they might have been overheard by the children.

"*Elle est pourrie, cette femme!*" Louise cried. "She's ruined the community with her immorality and her so-called open marriage. This sort of behaviour might be common in Rennes, but people don't want it going on here."

She was obviously talking about Solenn.

"What about you?" Tegwenn fired back.

Jennifer stopped breathing to listen. What was Louise up to?

"You've been protecting Madeleine ever since she started seeing Derek. And now Tristan is dead too! What has she told you?" Tegwenn demanded.

Jennifer heard a noise of drawers being opened and shut but couldn't make out Louise's reply, if there was one. She hoped that Louise wasn't looking for the carving knife. Unless it was Tegwenn.

"Oh my God, one of them is coming over here," Pippa whispered at the sound of the kitchen door being opened then slammed. "Quick, hide!"

They heard footsteps crossing the courtyard and the wooden door swung open on its hinges, almost crushing Pippa behind it. Jennifer stood like a statue behind a painting of Madeleine propped on an easel near the back, praying that whoever it was wouldn't come her way.

The light illuminated every corner of the studio. From her concealed position, Jennifer could make out Louise's figure. She began opening the drawers that Jennifer had inspected only minutes before, but clearly didn't find what she needed.

"*Merde!*" Louise exclaimed to herself. She went to the other side of the barn where she bent over some clutter, which she began moving around in her search. She stood up again and wiped her forehead.

From behind her easel, Jennifer glimpsed the ginger cat enter as though he owned the place. With his tail upright, she watched him, aghast, as he made his way straight towards her. A moment later she could feel his fur tickling her left leg.

"*Putain,*" Louise said, stretching her arms. Her voice disturbed the cat, who, still with his tail in the air, sauntered towards his mistress, who didn't seem pleased to see him.

"*Qu'est-ce que tu fais là?*" she demanded, pointing towards the open door. "*Dehors!*"

She turned and looked back towards the kitchen. A moment later, she walked out of the barn behind Genghis, pulling the door shut behind her.

Please don't lock it, Jennifer prayed.

"Let's get out of here," Pippa whispered. "That scared me stiff!"

"God, did you see the cat? I was terrified! He might have given the game away if he'd miaowed. But what about the photo?"

"Never mind. What we heard is even more interesting, don't you think? I mean, we've got the confirmation that Madeleine was seeing Derek. Now all we need is the motive . . ."

"Yes, but hearing a conversation isn't like proof, is it?"

Pippa held up her phone.

"I recorded it."

CHAPTER 47

The two of them crept back to the car in the darkness like a pair of conspirators.

"God, I hope Tegwenn didn't notice it on his way home," Jennifer said as they clambered in.

"Don't worry about him," said Pippa. "He wouldn't know it belongs to me anyway."

"Are you sure? Didn't they mention in the paper when Bucky was killed that this car had been spotted outside the bakery at the time of his death?"

Pippa started the car with a jolt and proceeded to do a three-point turn in the narrow lane.

"I told you, don't worry," she said. "Oh damn. Look who's there."

Walking along the other side of the road was the bespectacled figure of Christine, tugging her dog on a leash. She looked closely at the car to see who it was, and recognised Pippa.

"*Bonsoir*, Peeper!" she said. "What are you doing here?"

Pippa rolled down the window "Oh, we just called on friends," she replied. "See you soon!"

She pulled away, looking in the rearview mirror at Christine, who was standing there, perplexed.

"Oh no . . . So what happens now?" Jennifer wanted to know. "I'm getting nervous."

"Let's sleep on it. I'm obviously going to tell Yann, because I think what we've got could be actionable. But I also think that you should have a word with Louise. She's the key to this, don't you think?"

Jennifer sighed. "But I'm not going back there for two weeks. I'd need an excuse, wouldn't I? And anyway, it looks to me like she's protecting her friend, just like Tegwenn was suggesting."

"You just need an excuse to call round? Give her a ring and say you want to talk about Mariam's progress. She wouldn't suspect anything . . ."

Jennifer knew that Pippa was right, but she didn't want to hear. And what if Christine alerted Madeleine or Louise that she'd seen them?

"If Louise doesn't want to talk, though, the whole thing would come crashing down!" Jennifer protested. She didn't see why she was the one doing the investigating. "Isn't this a job for the police?" she protested.

Pippa shook her head as she turned into her cul de sac where Jennifer's car was parked outside her house. Jennifer got out and said to Pippa, "Like you said, let's sleep on it."

* * *

The next morning, Jennifer was still brooding about whether to get in touch with Louise. As she dropped hay over the fence into the sheep meadow, she thought that it could be counterproductive, alerting Louise to her and Pippa's suspicions.

By the time she reached the chicken run with a watering can in one hand and a bucket of grain in the other, she'd convinced herself that it was the right thing to do. She could easily explain that she wanted to discuss Mariam's progress.

She returned to the house, where Philippe was having breakfast with the children. She felt so grateful that he'd fitted in so well with their little household and seemed to have earned the children's respect.

"You've got five minutes before we leave for school, you two," she said. She rang Louise and arranged to call in on her that afternoon.

As she went to the sink to wash her hands, she remembered that she'd been invited to Meredith's the following night for dinner with Pippa and Solenn, for one of their regular get-togethers. She frowned. She couldn't ask Philippe to keep an eye on Luke and Mariam. He'd already agreed to help her prepare her chickens for market in the afternoon. What about asking Jonathan? She sighed. Maybe she'd ask Philippe after all.

She turned to face the table where he was slurping his coffee in a competition with Luke to see who could make the most noise.

"Philippe?" she said. He put down his coffee *bol* guiltily, as though he'd been caught out.

"I was just wondering whether you were thinking of staying at your place tomorrow night."

"I see." He grinned. "Yes, I was. Why?"

"It's just that I've been invited to Meredith's for one of our girls' nights . . . how would you feel about that?" she asked.

"You mean you're inviting me as an honorary girl?"

She laughed. "No. Not this time. I mean, how would you feel about staying here for the evening? I won't be late, and I'll leave you all a nice dinner."

"Oh, in that case . . ." he smiled. She'd tricked him into babysitting and he didn't seem to mind. She had no way of knowing whether he was speaking the truth, but she thanked him anyway.

"Come on, Luke, Mariam, get your things, we don't want to be late," she said.

* * *

Louise was pulling up weeds outside the front door when Jennifer stopped the car at the bottom of the garden.

She got up from her crouched position and stretched her back.

"I know how you feel," said Jennifer. "Welcome to my life. I have a smallholding, and weeding is a full-time occupation for me."

"Come in, come in," said Louise. "What a pity your English doctor friend died. He could have helped you with your back."

"Yes, I suppose so," Jennifer replied, following her into the front room. At least Louise hadn't mentioned Christine so far, so she felt confident that she could relax.

"Tea? You Brits always like the five o'clock tea, I think? Although it's only three, so maybe not . . ." She looked at Jennifer quizzically.

"If you're making some, that would be fine," said Jennifer with a smile. Sometimes she found these conversations comparing life in Britain and France rather tedious.

Jennifer followed Louise into the kitchen where she poured water into a small pan on the hob. Like most of the Bretons Jennifer knew, Louise didn't have a kettle. Jennifer wondered how to broach the issue of Madeleine and realised that Louise had already given her an opening.

"Talking of our friend Derek, did you know that he was having an affair with Madeleine?"

Louise, who was pouring hot water over a tea bag in a mug, put the pan down and stared at her in surprise. Then she turned back to what she was doing, apparently wondering how to respond.

"Milk?" she asked.

"Yes, just a drop." Louise took out some milk and prepared to heat it on the stove.

"No, cold is fine. Thanks," said Jennifer.

"So, you ask about Derek. Madeleine was not in a happy marriage and she was seeing him. But he finished with her.

She was very upset. She told me they had a big argument but he insisted it was over."

Had she been so upset that she might have wanted to kill him? Jennifer wondered.

"And did you mention this to the police? You see, she was one of Derek's fitness clients who would have had a class on the day he died."

Louise hesitated before replying. "Madeleine asked me not to mention it and I respected her wishes," she said.

So Louise had been protecting her friend, just like Tegwenn had suggested, Jennifer realised. She was about to ask another question when Louise said, "I thought you wanted to talk to me about Mariam?"

"Mariam? Oh yes I do," said Jennifer.

"Actually, I think you'd better go now," said Louise.

CHAPTER 48

Jennifer produced an early supper for Philippe and the children before leaving home the next evening.

She'd bought some pâté for Philippe and Luke on the way home from the school run, and roasted a chicken because she knew that Philippe was always hungry after plucking chickens. They'd deal with the leftovers later in the week. Mariam said she'd make her own avocado on toast, and was happy to have a homemade apple crumble. As for Luke, he'd realised he could help himself to as much ice cream as he wanted.

When Jennifer headed out to Meredith's the children were upstairs and Philippe stretched out on the sofa with his feet on the coffee table, flicking through the TV channels with the remote. She hugged him from behind the couch, and thanked him again.

"I won't be late — promise," she said.

"Take the Camembert if you like, from the kitchen counter," he said, before she set off.

Jennifer pulled up outside Meredith's converted farmhouse a few minutes later, just as Pippa arrived, carrying a bottle of wine and a warm baguette. So the two of them were able to run the gauntlet together of Meredith's Collie cross who always tried to round up guests.

Meredith appeared at the front door after obviously hearing the barking and the squealing of the two women. Two carved pumpkins sat on each side, with candles lighting up their smiles from inside.

"Captain!" she commanded, pointing at his kennel, and he slunk off in their ritual which must have been repeated several times every day.

"Maybe he could smell this?" said Jennifer, holding up the cheese.

Meredith led the way into the dark wood-panelled dining room, where Solenn was already seated with a drink in her hand.

"How are you all? It's been ages," said Pippa, as they took their places while Meredith filled their glasses. Pippa held up a hand and said, "Not for me, thanks," when her turn arrived. Jennifer looked across at her in surprise, and Pippa said, "Early morning tomorrow" by way of explanation.

"It's just a simple supper," Meredith said, apologetically. "Have some nuts. I've got quite a lot on at the moment."

Everyone turned to face her. "How's it going? Are the other councillors more cooperative?" Pippa asked.

"Ha!" Meredith replied. "That will never happen. No, we're basically divided into two camps. Not for political reasons. But half of the council is aligned with Christine, one of my deputies, and the other half with me and Erwan, the first deputy."

Her hooded eyes darkened. "It's exhausting, actually. It's practically impossible to reach a conclusion along practical lines. There's always someone from the other camp who raises their hand to object. I'm sure Sylvie puts them up to it."

"Sylvie is close to Christine, right?" Pippa asked.

Meredith nodded. "Unfortunately, yes."

She got up and went into the kitchen. Jennifer suspected when she smelled the aroma through the open door that Meredith had roasted one of her chickens. When she returned to the dining room, she served the broiler with roast potatoes and green beans tossed with garlic.

"This is delicious," said Solenn, slicing into her chicken breast and tasting a tiny bit on her fork. Meredith gave Jennifer a wink across the table.

"What news of the investigation?" said Meredith, turning to Solenn. "I've not seen anything in the paper recently."

Solenn put down her fork. "Nothing. No. I'm afraid not. It's very disappointing. But the investigators are looking into the possibility that it was the same person who killed Derek and Tristan."

"Oh," said Jennifer. "I heard on the grapevine that Madeleine, Tristan's wife, was having an affair with Derek."

Solenn looked genuinely surprised. Jennifer remembered that she'd always said that the two of them never discussed their relationships outside the marriage.

"Really?" Solenn said. "I wonder what he could have seen in her."

"Well," said Pippa. "She was one of his fitness clients."

"Ah yes," Solenn replied. "And now she's lost her husband as well. Sad."

The table fell silent as they all kept their thoughts to themselves, although Pippa flashed a meaningful look at Jennifer. Then Pippa turned to Meredith and said, "Your Christine on the council was another of Derek's fitness clients."

"Yes, I know," said Meredith. "She told me that he helped her with a bad back."

Pippa glanced across at Jennifer, who had an odd look on her face.

Pippa checked her watch. It was time for her to go or she'd never get up at 4 a.m. Jennifer got up with her and they left together.

"What's up?" Pippa asked as they made their way to their cars after Meredith had waved them off from the front door.

"You know when you knead dough?" she asked. "Do you wear disposable gloves?"

"Yes, of course. For hygiene, and they also stop the dough sticking to your fingers. I sometimes wear them for serving customers too."

"Because I've just remembered a portrait of Madeleine that Louise is working on. It shows her kneading dough in the back room of the bakery."

"And she's wearing gloves? So what?" Pippa asked.

"I just thought that if you're going to commit a murder with a baguette, you wouldn't want your fingerprints on it, would you? And it would be dead easy to dispose of the gloves afterwards."

"I see what you mean," said Pippa. "So no DNA!"

CHAPTER 49

Yann looked across the kitchen table at Pippa and sighed.

"Peeper, what have you done now?" he said. It was a couple of nights later and they were having pancakes that Yann had prepared. Pippa's favourite was the *galette complète* of cheese and ham, topped with an egg.

"Like I say, we're just joining up the dots." She pointed to her phone on the table.

Yann had listened to the recording in silence. Luckily its contents temporarily eclipsed the circumstances in which it had been made. Pippa had glossed over the fact that she and Jennifer had broken into private property, and she suggested that they'd heard voices while standing outside in Louise's courtyard. And what better way to react than to record the row between the couple, which seemed to cast light on the murder inquiry?

"From this conversation we know that Madeleine — who was a client of Derek's — was in a romantic relationship with him. She's also the wife of Tristan, who was found dead in his bakery. As for the breadcrumbs at the murder scene, I recall that there was no DNA in the case of either Derek or Tristan, was there?"

"Well, as you will remember, in both cases, the incriminating baguettes were thrown into the stream, making it very hard to detect fingerprints," Yann replied. "What you're saying could be circumstantial."

Pippa replied, "We have seen a painting in which Madeleine has gloves on while making bread. Like any good baker she'd have had an endless supply of them, so no fingerprints makes perfect sense — and wouldn't it have been easy to throw them away after the murder? The only thing we don't know yet is the motive!"

Yann stroked his chin as he always did when weighing evidence. To Pippa's surprise he didn't ask what the two of them had been doing in Louise's courtyard in the first place.

"And that's your job, isn't it, finding the motive?" Pippa went on. "Nice galette, thank you."

"It's true that the mode of killing points to the same murderer. And you're right that Madeleine is a person with a connection to both of the victims. But from there to conclude that she is the murderer . . ." He raised his arms in a Gallic shrug and looked to heaven.

"Yes, but this is good background, isn't it, for you to question her?"

"She has been questioned, Peeper, and she pointed the finger at you," he said, grimly.

"You mean by lying about my car?"

"There is also the question of the breadcrumbs," he said, shaking his head slowly. "Do you also wear gloves when making bread?"

Pippa pursed her lips. She couldn't believe that Yann would suspect her for a second.

He reached out and took her hand. "I'm joking, of course," he said, quickly.

"Well, there's also a possible second suspect, with connections to Derek and Tristan Trobellec. It's Christine, the second deputy at the *mairie*."

"And the motive?"

"Isn't that your job?" she said again, leaning towards him.

He smiled. "Leave this with me. But Peeper, you must stop this freelance investigating because already you have a certain reputation."

He looked at her and frowned. "I'm serious," he said.

"Of course," she replied.

CHAPTER 50

Pippa had a sleepless night, turning over the theories in her mind.

It was possible that the murderer was Christine, who fulfilled the criteria that had narrowed down their informal investigation.

But it was Madeleine who now stood out as the prime suspect. Pippa felt betrayed by her. The woman had clearly befriended her in order to throw her off the scent. Now that they were sure she'd been a client of Derek as well as his lover, there was no doubt in Pippa's mind that she and Jennifer had found the culprit in both murders.

She also wrestled with Yann's warning. Did she dare defy him? When the alarm rang, she was dreaming of a portrait of Madeleine in which the real Madeleine seemed to step out of the painting to strangle her. She woke up with a jump to get ready for work.

Once at the bakery, she switched on the radio and dealt with the tasks at hand as though on automatic pilot. She took the baguettes and croissants out of the proofer and put them in the oven. By the time 8 a.m. came along, all the bread and cakes were arranged in time for the first customer.

Pippa had a plan. She waited until Gwen arrived for her shift at ten and asked her to hold the fort for about half an hour.

Fifteen minutes later, she pulled up outside Madeleine's bakery in Ploumenel and went in. She was the only customer.

"*Bonjour*, Madeleine," she said, breezily. "I was thinking about the olive loaves you mentioned some time ago, and I thought I might try one."

Madeleine smiled. "You're in luck, Peeper, I have four of them this morning."

"I'll just take one, thanks . . . are you on your own? You're not hiring an apprentice?" Pippa took out her card to pay, swiping it on the automatic till.

"As you know, it's not easy to find a good one, and we only let go of our last apprentice a few weeks ago," Madeleine replied. "To be honest, I'm wondering whether to keep the shop. I might move."

Was she thinking of leaving the neighbourhood? Fleeing the scene of her crimes? This was a vital piece of information, Pippa thought, but didn't question her further. She wondered whether to mention Bucky but thought better of it.

Instead, she said, "Maybe you could recommend a good yoga teacher, by the way? I know that you were a client of Derek, and I want to take a class."

She emphasised the word "client", possibly too much, because Madeleine's expression changed as her face froze and her eyes flashed hatred across the counter. *She knows the game is up*, thought Pippa.

"No I can't, I'm afraid," she replied, recovering her composure.

"Oh. Never mind," said Pippa, as pleasantly as she could manage. "*Bonne journée!* See you at the market tomorrow!"

She walked out to her car as fast as she could, carrying her olive loaf. *Two can play at that game*, she thought to herself.

CHAPTER 51

The next morning, Pippa was in the back room of the bakery bent over her bread and pastries when she heard the outside door behind her.

It was too early for Gwen, and in any case she always used the front entrance.

"I thought I'd find you here, you *pétasse!*" It was Madeleine.

Pippa wasn't used to being called a bitch so early in the morning. She could almost see the steam coming out of Madeleine's ears. Pippa had expected her to react in some way, but not necessarily so soon, nor so crudely.

Pippa blinked. Then, adopting a polite attitude in the hope of defusing the situation, she said calmly, "*Bonjour*, Madeleine. Is something the matter?"

"Something the matter?" Madeleine threw back at her. "I hear you've been sniffing around in Ploumenel trying to pin my husband's murder on me!"

"I'm sorry, I've done no such thing," said Pippa. "And now, if you don't mind, I have to get ready for market. And I think that you should too."

"So how come your car was parked in Ploumenel the day before yesterday, near Louise's house?" Madeleine demanded.

Pippa immediately realised it must have been Christine who had reported her. No doubt Madeleine had also been fully briefed by now on Louise's conversation with Jennifer. Therefore her visit must have been prompted by the realisation of how much Pippa knew, after she'd gone to her bakery the day before. It was all starting to make sense. But Pippa wasn't going to take this lying down.

She folded her arms and said, "It turns out that I happen to know that you attempted to pin your husband's murder on me by falsely asserting that my car was parked outside the bakery at the time of his death!"

She added, "And I would remind you that it was your husband who wrongly accused me of cutting off the electricity in his bakery, which turned out to have been done by an employee.

"I don't know what you've got against me, but you've undermined my reputation in this village and have made me fear for the future of my business," Pippa went on. "In fact, you and your friends have done everything you can to make me feel unwelcome here. I've even received a poison pen letter accusing me of having killed Madame Briand with one of my baguettes. And another thing, thinking about it now, I bet it was you who sent it to destroy my business, all the while pretending to be my friend. It's outrageous!"

Madeleine didn't respond, but stood her ground with a glare, convincing Pippa even more of her guilt.

"Did you know when you sent it that Madame Briand had been poisoned?"

"What are you talking about, you stupid woman? How could I have known that when I wrote the letter? I only heard that she'd choked on a baguette and so I knew it must have been one of yours!"

Oops, thought Pippa. *What a surprise confession.*

Madeleine was working herself into a greater frenzy.

"How dare you!" she said. "You think you can come over here and open a bakery without any consideration for the rest of us who have worked our fingers to the bone all our lives. We're the ones whose business is suffering! What about your market stall? You only opened it to steal our customers!"

"Don't be ridiculous!" Pippa shouted. She was struck that Madeleine was using almost identical language to the insults spat out by her husband earlier.

"You and your fancy ways, with your special cakes and whatnot."

"You mean my *tropéziennes*? As I told your husband, I'm only baking the cakes that my customers appreciate. And there's nothing to stop you doing that either, instead of your stodgy Far Bretons and pathetic olive bread. The one you sold me yesterday was soggy, by the way."

Pippa realised she may have gone too far with her criticism of the local fare. It seemed to be the last straw for Madeleine. "Anyway," she responded, "I'm not going to put up with it anymore, and I'll teach you a lesson, you police informant!"

She took out a baguette from a tote bag on her shoulder and brandished it like a weapon.

Pippa turned to the shelf behind her and picked out a *tradition*. *If that's the way she wants it, it'll be baguettes at dawn*, she thought.

Madeleine raised her arm to thwack her baguette against Pippa's head, but Pippa ducked the blow and instead it hit her around the waist. She stumbled back against the shelves from the force of the blow, and could feel that her side must be bruised. This was no ordinary baguette.

In turn, she brought her own loaf down on Madeleine's shoulder. The bread broke in half. Madeleine approached Pippa, an evil glint in her eyes, holding up her baguette.

Pippa knew instantly that the baguette murderer was standing in front of her. Did her loaf contain the same type of metal rod that had killed Derek and Bucky? She didn't wait to find out. She grabbed as many croissants as she could in both hands and chucked them straight at Madeleine, who lost her balance. Pippa then pushed her to the ground, where she fell onto her side with a grunt.

As Madeleine struggled to her feet, Pippa snatched the baguette weapon from her and threw it into a corner. She took her phone out of her trouser pocket and called Yann's number. He answered straight away. "Come to the bakery now!" she pleaded before Madeleine grabbed her from behind and began pulling her hair.

Pippa screamed. She managed to turn round to face Madeleine, whose face was twisted with hatred, and shook her by both arms. Pippa noticed her opponent's eyes searching in all directions before she pushed Pippa away and picked up a blade from the bench where Pippa laminated croissant dough.

She held it up, threateningly. Pippa wasn't sure whether she was going to hurt her or use it to back out of the door and escape, but she could feel her legs trembling beneath her.

She reached behind and opened the fridge door, picking up a *tropézienne* and throwing it straight at Madeleine's face. The whipped cream stuck to her cheeks and caught in her hair, making her look like a circus clown. *What a waste of a good cake*, Pippa thought.

The back door was pushed open and there stood Yann, in his blue uniform. He immediately took in the scene. Madeleine, surprised, dropped the blade onto the bench when he said, "Put that down."

"Yann Berthou, *adjudant-chef de la gendarmerie*," he announced.

Pippa motioned to the tampered baguette lying in the corner. Yann nodded when he saw it.

"Madeleine Trobellec, you're coming with me on suspicion of murdering Derek Cooper and Tristan Trobellec. And on a charge of assaulting Madame Pippa Sinclair with a lethal weapon."

Turning to Pippa, he said, gently, "Don't touch anything here. Someone will come."

He led Madeleine outside by the arm, explaining that she had a right to silence, leaving Pippa winded and in tears.

She took out her phone again and called Jennifer.

"Hello," said Jennifer in her cheerful voice. "Everything OK? I'm driving to the market. See you there?"

"I need to tell you something," said Pippa, sobbing. "I'm just waiting for the gendarmes to come to the bakery."

"Hang on, let me pull over. Now tell me."

Pippa blurted out the details of Madeleine's attack and Yann's arrival in the nick of time.

"Do you need me to stop on my way?" Jennifer asked. "I'm only two minutes away."

Pippa was waiting for her outside the bakery when she parked her car outside the *mairie*.

"Wait till you see this," said Pippa, leading her behind the counter so they could see into the back room.

"We can't go in," Pippa said.

Jennifer surveyed the chaos of the smashed croissants, breadcrumbs and whipped cream all over the floor, the laminating bench pushed to one side and the fridge door hanging open.

"Wow. Bunfight at the OK Corral," she deadpanned.

CHAPTER 52

Jennifer left for the market, promising to return on her way home.

Pippa pulled down the bakery shutters and turned the shop sign to *Closed*. She rang Gwen and told her that she wouldn't need her services that day. She hadn't had time to put her wares on display in the bakery, and the back room was now off limits. Two gendarmes were making lists of things and they said forensics were on their way. They promised to call her as soon as they finished.

She walked home slowly and unsteadily, having left the car at the bakery. Now that the adrenalin had dissipated, she felt bone tired and could feel a throbbing bruise where Madeleine had hit her. Raising a hand to rub her head, the scalp was sensitive after having her hair pulled. She'd better see her doctor to get checked out, she thought.

A rush of conflicting feelings swirled in her brain. She was torn between anger and sorrow. What Madeleine's visit had proved to her was how, under a veneer of politeness, the locals resented her presence and probably that of the other Brits in the neighbourhood. It was something that Meredith had often talked about, but Pippa was shocked by the series of incidents in which she'd been targeted. Should she stay to confront her enemies, or throw in the towel?

She reached her house and unlocked the door. She went upstairs to run herself a hot bath, where she usually did her thinking. She stretched out in the warm water and tried to relax.

She began a mental inventory to help her decide. Uprooting herself again was such a big decision. On the upside, there was Yann, Jennifer and her lovely neighbours. Then Meredith and Erwan on the council, and Michel and Solange from the bar-tabac. How could she forget Gwen at the bakery? But how long would she stay? And what about Solenn, who'd always been on the fringes of her local friendships. She dabbed her face with a cloth and ran some more hot water to refresh the bath. Then she considered the negatives, starting with Sylvie and Christine. She'd made enemies of Bucky and Madeleine at the market, and knew all too well the repercussions that had followed from that . . . She sank deeper into the bathwater as she contemplated a possible return to London. Or a move to Manchester, where her daughters were. But once there, wouldn't she be lonely? And anywhere she went there would still be the good, the bad and the ugly, just like here. Not to mention financing such a move which would test her resources. What about Yann? He would surely visit, wouldn't he? Lots of people had long distance relationships these days.

She sighed and stepped out of the bath, pulling a towel round her. Is this what they call a mid-life crisis? she thought.

* * *

Pippa's doorbell rang just after lunch. She hoped it might be Yann with some news, but instead she saw Jennifer wearing a concerned look on her face.

"How are you doing?" she asked.

"I guess it only hit me afterwards, but that mad cow might have killed me," said Pippa with a rueful smile. "Otherwise, I'm fine. Do you want a cuppa?"

The two of them went into the kitchen where Pippa put the kettle on.

"The market was quiet today," Jennifer said. "Neither you nor Madeleine. Meredith asked me what was going on but I didn't go into detail. She'll find out soon enough."

"If it turns out that the baguette that Madeleine tried to kill me with actually was stuffed with a metal rod, it's obvious that she was the murderer of both Derek and her husband."

Jennifer accepted a mug of steaming Earl Grey and sat at the kitchen table. She nodded.

"I can understand why she would have killed Derek — I mean, revenge, love, maybe even jealousy if she knew about him having multiple sexual partners. I suppose that it was one thing for Derek and Solenn to have consensual affairs. But maybe their lovers didn't feel the same way . . . But why Bucky? And why so much later?"

"I agree," said Pippa. "I don't get that either. And wasn't it weird that she came after me like that? As if she didn't mind being caught? She'd obviously lost her mind and didn't care. It strikes me that she knew the game was up after I challenged her at the bakery yesterday."

Pippa told Jennifer about how she'd defied Yann's caution and confronted Madeleine.

"You didn't?" said Jennifer. "You told her we knew she and Derek were lovers?"

Pippa grimaced. "Not exactly. I just mentioned that I knew she was one of his *clients*. Do you think that's what pushed her over the edge?" She joined Jennifer at the table.

"Could be," said Jennifer, staring into her mug. "Also, Louise told me that Madeleine and Bucky weren't happily married, which is presumably why she went off with Derek. Hopefully Yann will be able to cast light on the situation," she added.

"I was surprised that when he arrested Madeleine, he came in with the actual charges of suspected murder. He hadn't even seen the killer baguette until I pointed it out to him."

"Really? That's interesting," Jennifer mused, cupping her hands round her mug.

"It makes me think that the gendarmerie acted on what I told him earlier, or maybe they'd found out for themselves, you never know," said Pippa with a smile. "Do you think it odd that Madeleine killed Bucky with a metal rod inside a baguette? And that's what she used on me too . . ."

"No, not at all. I think she was clever. I'm sure she was trying to pin Bucky's murder on you by using the same technique as for Derek," Jennifer replied.

"Right. But then why come for me with the same thing again?"

"Because, as a baker, it was her weapon of choice, wasn't it? She must have thought in her sick mind that she'd got away with two murders, so why change horses midstream if you're onto a winner?"

Pippa sighed. "Oh my God . . ."

"So now what?" said Jennifer.

"I've been thinking about that. Do you know, I'm not sure I want to stay here." Pippa pulled a face and had to stop herself from crying.

"What? What are you talking about? Of course you must stay! You've got the best bakery in the neighbourhood and everybody loves you."

Pippa frowned. "Do you really think so? Madeleine definitely had it in for me, but now she's gone. But what about Christine and Sylvie at the *mairie*? Do I have to keep on seeing those acid-faced women right across from my bakery? As well as Christine's damned dog?"

"But they can't harm you. And anyway, Meredith's on their case." Jennifer put an arm round Pippa to console her. "Come on. This isn't like you. You've solved a murder and you shouldn't run away on an impulse. You'll feel better soon, you'll see. And don't forget Yann. Isn't he a good reason to stay?"

CHAPTER 53

Pippa ran to the door when the doorbell sounded at eight o'clock.

Yann was outside, still in his uniform, beaming. She took him by the arm to lead him into the hall where they embraced.

"Are you OK, Peeper?" he asked, stepping back and looking at her closely. "You were very brave today. Madeleine is going to prison for a very long time."

"Can you tell me what she said? I mean, she obviously came to the bakery to try to kill me with that stupid baguette stuffed with metal. She really hurt me."

Pippa stroked the bruise on her side as she remembered the attack.

"Are you alright?"

"Yes. Thank you. The doctor says it's only bruising."

"This information is confidential, as you know, but she confessed everything," said Yann.

Pippa nodded her head vigorously. Madeleine had been caught red-handed in the bakery, after all.

"It was as you told me. Madeleine was having an affair with Derek and couldn't tolerate losing him when he ended it. That was the first death."

"OK. I suppose the reason being that if she couldn't have him, nobody could." Yann's facial expression suggested that he thought she was right.

"She didn't say that in so many words, but yes. The reason that she started the affair with Derek, though, was because her husband was refusing to give her a divorce."

"Ah. But then why would she go on to kill him? I don't understand," said Pippa.

"It seems that Tristan Trobellec had discovered about the affair with Derek Cooper, and when she told him that it was over, he realised that she must have killed him. He was threatening to denounce her to the gendarmerie and that made her react by stopping him before he could do that." He shook his head. "The only way she could think of to prevent him from tipping us off, was by killing him."

"I see. Because the first murder hadn't been solved, possibly? She must have thought that she could get away with it a second time . . ."

"Maybe, maybe not," said Yann.

Had he been stung by her suggestion, she wondered.

"Anyway, Madeleine's version has been corroborated by her friend Louise. We'd already called her in to revise her original statement, in which she didn't appear to have given the full version of what she knew. After your friend Derek was killed, Louise was suspicious that Madeleine had also murdered her husband. She made the connection too, you see, but she never believed that Madeleine would have been capable of such a thing. And so the charges had already been drawn up when you rang me this morning. Little did I know that Madeleine was intending to strike again!"

"So Louise had been protecting her all along, just like we thought," said Pippa. "And to think that if Jennifer hadn't taken Mariam there for art classes, we'd never have found out!"

Yann seemed puzzled. "So that is how you knew Louise?"

"That's how Jennifer knows her, yes," said Pippa, without providing further explanation for fear of digging herself into a deeper hole. "And now what are you doing?" she asked.

Yann gestured towards his uniform. "As you can see, it's been a long day. I'm going to have a shower and then something to eat. Do you want to join me?"

"Actually, no. Not tonight. It's been a long day for me too, and I need to try to sleep it off," she replied.

* * *

A couple of days later, Pippa picked up *Le Télégramme* from the bar-tabac. The bakery, now a crime scene, was still closed and she wasn't expecting to be able to reopen until the end of the week. But she wasn't displeased to have some unexpected time off.

Michel, the ruddy-faced owner, greeted her warmly. "*Bonjour*, Peeper . . . Madeleine, eh? Who'd have thought?"

She grinned. "Yes, indeed."

Michel seemed to have something on his mind, and she ordered an espresso at the bar. She wasn't in a rush.

"Do you know what?" Michel said. "When I heard about Madeleine being the double murderer, I remembered once when she and Derek came in here. They sat in the corner there—" he pointed towards a table — "and she seemed upset about something. Or even angry."

Pippa, sipping her coffee, put down her cup onto the saucer with a bang. Hadn't Solenn once mentioned that Derek used to come to the café after his yoga class?

"Didn't you tell that to the police?" she asked. What if he'd witnessed the very moment that Derek had finished with Madeleine, which had triggered the murder?

He shrugged. "They did come round. But no, I didn't mention Madeleine specifically. Why would I? I'd never suspect her of murdering anyone! And then, when Tristan was killed, I felt sorry for her. Wouldn't everyone? And then it turned out that she murdered him too! I mean, it's incredible!"

Pippa didn't know whether to laugh or cry. Wouldn't the police have been the best judge of that information?

She felt a flash of resentment at how much time could have been saved if Michel had come forward with what he had witnessed.

But it was too late to worry about that now. She found a twenty euro note in her jacket pocket and asked, "How much do I owe you?"

Back at the house, she turned the pages of the newspaper until she reached the Louennec page. The top story described how "heroic" baker Pippa Sinclair had fought off suspected murderer Madeleine Trobellec, who had confessed to two murders in the *commune*.

The article said that Pippa ran a "popular bakery" and was famous for her "legendary" *tropéziennes*. She had to read that sentence twice, smiling at the thought that maybe Jennifer had planted the quotes in the paper. But still, if she got more customers as a result, who was she to complain?

During the rest of the day she occupied herself by baking some chocolate chip cookies before taking the car out to the supermarket for supplies. She pushed four of the biscuits through the front door of Morgane's house with a little note. Later, she caught up on her catering invoices and other administrative chores which she'd let slip.

Her phone rang at about six. She was surprised to see that it was Michel, the bar-tabac owner, and worried that something else might have happened. He wasn't in the habit of ringing her.

She answered somewhat hesitantly and his loud voice boomed over the phone: "*Re-bonjour*, Peeper. Ca *va*?"

"Ca *va*," she said, still apprehensive. "Ca *va, toi*?"

"*Oui*, ca *va*." They could now move on to the point of his call. "Do you remember when you came in this morning? You left some money here. Can you come over to pick it up?"

Pippa felt in her pockets absent-mindedly. On the rare occasions that she paid in cash, that's where she put the change.

"Are you sure it was me?" she said.

"Oh yes. You paid for your paper and coffee in cash, and didn't wait for the change from twenty euros. Solange just mentioned it to me. Otherwise we would have rung you earlier."

"I see. Thank you." Pippa had to admit she'd been distracted that morning, after all.

She took her handbag from the kitchen table and walked round to the café. When she pushed open the door, she was practically floored by the number of people inside. It was only when everyone shouted "Surprise!" that she realised what was going on.

Pippa's hand flew up to her face, not knowing whether to laugh or cry. Jennifer was there, of course, arm in arm with Philippe. She caught sight of Gwen, her apprentice. Meredith had brought her new deputy, Gwen's brother Erwan. Solenn stood at the bar, smiling broadly. Pippa also recognised her neighbours and about a dozen of her customers, although she didn't know them by name. And standing at the back was Monsieur le curé, who was talking to Yann.

Pippa looked over the bar at Michel and wagged a finger at him. "You shouldn't have done this, but thank you," she said.

"Thank you, our heroine baker," he said with a big grin. "What would you like? It's on the house. *Une coupe?*"

"Why not?" she said. She felt like celebrating the end of her nightmare with a glass of champagne. Michel handed it over, and she held up the glass in a toast.

"Thank you, everyone. I can't tell you how kind this is of you."

Jennifer stepped forward. "So you're not leaving then?"

Pippa's eyes were pricked by tears. "No, I'm staying," she said, looking straight at Yann. And everyone clapped.

THE END

ACKNOWLEDGEMENTS

I owe a huge debt of gratitude to Brigitte Vallée and to Céline Tran, whose rich experiences inspired me to create the fictional characters of Jennifer and Pippa in this series of Brittany murders. I'm also very grateful to my friends Margaret Crompton and Peter Kessler for their invaluable advice, and, as ever, to my wonderful editors at Joffe Books.

THE JOFFE BOOKS STORY

We began in 2014 when Jasper agreed to publish his mum's much-rejected romance novel and it became a bestseller.

Since then we've grown into the largest independent publisher in the UK. We're extremely proud to publish some of the very best writers in the world, including Joy Ellis, Faith Martin, Caro Ramsay, Helen Forrester, Simon Brett and Robert Goddard. Everyone at Joffe Books loves reading and we never forget that it all begins with the magic of an author telling a story.

We are proud to publish talented first-time authors, as well as established writers whose books we love introducing to a new generation of readers.

We won Trade Publisher of the Year at the Independent Publishing Awards in 2023 and Best Publisher Award in 2024 at the People's Book Prize. We have been shortlisted for Independent Publisher of the Year at the British Book Awards for the last five years, and were shortlisted for the Diversity and Inclusivity Award at the 2022 Independent Publishing Awards. In 2023 we were shortlisted for Publisher of the Year at the RNA Industry Awards, and in 2024 we were shortlisted at the CWA Daggers for the Best Crime and Mystery Publisher.

We built this company with your help, and we love to hear from you, so please email us about absolutely anything bookish at feedback@joffebooks.com.

If you want to receive free books every Friday and hear about all our new releases, join our mailing list here: www.joffebooks.com/freebooks.

And when you tell your friends about us, just remember: it's pronounced Joffe as in coffee or toffee!

www.ingramcontent.com/pod-product-compliance
Ingram Content Group UK Ltd.
Pitfield, Milton Keynes, MK11 3LW, UK
UKHW021307220125
4239UKWH00047B/1143

9 781835 269732